Francis Mading Deng was born in 1938 at Noong, near Abyei, the administrative center of the Ngok Dinka of whom his father was paramount chief. He attended elementary and intermediate schools in the southern Sudan and received his secondary education in the north. He was graduated from Khartoum University in 1962 and appointed to the university's faculty of law.

Dr. Deng has traveled extensively and has lived in Europe and the United States. He holds a doctorate in law from Yale University and has also studied in England. He has been an adjunct professor of law and anthropology at New York University and a visiting lecturer in law at Columbia University Law School. Dr. Deng is now serving as Sudan's ambassador to Scandinavia. Prior to that appointment he was an officer in the human rights division of the United Nations Secretariat.

Dr. Deng has published numerous articles on law and related fields in African, Asian, European, and American journals and is the author of *Tradition and Modernization: A Challenge for Law Among the Dinka of the Sudan* (Yale University Press, 1971) and *The Dinka of the Sudan* (Holt, Rinehart & Winston, 1972); he is also the translator and editor of the recently published *The Dinka and Their Songs. Tradition and Modernization* received the Herskovits Award, given each year by the African Studies Association "to a distinguished volume of research on Africa."

# DINKA FOLKTALES
African Stories from the Sudan

# DINKA FOLKTALES

## AFRICAN STORIES FROM THE SUDAN

BY

## Francis Mading Deng

*Illustrations by Martha Reisman*

Africana Publishing Company, A DIVISION OF
Holmes & Meier Publishers NEW YORK · LONDON

Published in the United States of America 1974 by
Africana Publishing Company, a Division of Holmes & Meier Publishers, Inc.
101 Fifth Avenue
New York, N.Y. 10003

Published in Great Britain 1974 by
Holmes & Meier Publishers, Ltd.
Hillview House
1, Hallswelle Parade, Finchley Road
London, N.W. 11 ODL

**Library of Congress Cataloging in Publication Data**

Deng, Francis Mading, 1938–
  Dinka folktales; African stories from the Sudan

  1. Tales, Dinka. Title. I.
GR360.D5D4613    398.2'09624    73–82901
ISBN 0-8419-0138-4

Designed by Paula Wiener

Printed in the United States of America

*To my dear wife,*
*Dorothy*

# Preface

The tales included in this volume are translations of original material recorded among the Dinka of the Sudan. Ethnically and culturally, the Dinka are Nilotic, akin to the Luo-speaking peoples of the Sudan and Uganda but with close affinities to the Nuer.* They are cattle herders and subsistence cultivators. Numbering about two million in a country of fifteen million people and over five hundred tribes, they are the largest tribal group in the Sudan. Their settlement covers one-tenth of the Sudan, a country of nearly one million square miles, the largest in Africa.

Cutting across this territory is the Nile and its tributaries, which frequently flood the country and render communication very difficult, if not impossible. As a result, Dinka settlements and, therefore, tribes are quite scattered and isolated from one another. Although improvements in modern education and communication have now made the Dinka more aware of each other, very few Dinka know all their tribes. Some tribes consider themselves *the* Dinka and call the others by their tribal names or by other differentiating, even derogatory, terms.

But although the Dinka are a congeries of some twenty-five mutually independent groups, they have a lot in common: their physical appearance, their cultural uniformity, and their pride in their race and culture. Despite the environmental hardships of their land, they love their country and, until recently, going to a foreign land was frowned upon and very rare. As they see it, God has been generous to them. They possess cattle, sheep, and goats and grow a wide variety of crops. Their rivers and lagoons teem with fish and their land with game. There are many kinds of wild crops, vegetables, and fruits in their natural environment. Honey is in plenty. Their

---

* It has been argued that the Nilotics are an admixture of Negroid and non-Negroid elements—Hamitic-Caucasian according to Professor C. G. Seligman. See his article, "Some Aspects of the Hamitic Problem in the Anglo-Egyptian Sudan," *Journal of the Royal Anthropological Institute*, 1913.

skies and pools are marvellously decorated with birds of every color, shape and size. Against the dangers of their hostile environment, the Dinka build huts for themselves and cattle-byres for their herds. Their walls of wood and mud and their roofs of rafters and grass have won great admiration from many observers.

The Dinka now form part of modern Sudan. They are among those of the Sudan less transformed by the impact of modernization. Their ethnocentrism has always been given as an important factor in their conservatism and resistance to change.* Post-colonial trends, however, now indicate that this explanation is only a partial truth. Colonial policies kept traditional societies isolated and tried to preserve their cultures. The abandonment of those policies has now led to intensive cross-cultural interaction. As a result of this and of modern education, the Dinka are demonstrating an adaptability to change that was never predicted. Although a certain continuity is inevitable, change, whatever its form, threatens traditional culture with a degree of extinction. This threat is particularly acute in the case of folklore, which age, education, and disaffiliation from the traditional environment tend to erase.

But although change tends to militate against traditional culture, the old pride of the Nilotics in their racial and cultural identity continues. The educated Dinka tends to be blind and even openly hostile to tradition, but he is deeply conscious of it. In my research, both inside the Sudan and abroad, I have found that all Dinka, including the educated, deeply enjoy talking, discussing, reminiscing and even bragging about the essential virtues of their people and their culture. Yet very few are aware of the fact that verbalized romanticism is not enough to save what is good in their culture. During this transitional period of political preoccupation and seeming denial of tradition, a great deal is being lost which could enrich the modern society of the Nilotics and the Sudan. When this loss is finally felt, the substance may no longer be there to find.

Of course, traditional society is bound to wither away in the course of time. But wittingly or unwittingly, the Nilotics and other traditional peoples are bound to take with them into the mainstream of modern Sudanese and

---

* A point which has been observed about cattle-raising peoples in general and the Nilotics in particular. See, for instance, C. G. and B. Z. Seligman, *Pagan Tribes of Nilotic Sudan* (1932) and Audrey Butt, *The Nilotics of the Anglo-Egyptian Sudan and Uganda* (1952).

world communities some of those values, sentiments and characteristics which they hold dear or cannot shed. The value of this selection could be enhanced if the cultural resources from which to choose were available and well articulated. In a sense, recording Dinka folktales is not only a preservation of what was and what is, it is an attempt to enrich what will be.

Despite their fantasies, their allegedly ancient origin, and the mysterious circumstances of their delivery, these tales reveal Dinka social realities in a dramatic combination of ideals and the drastic consequences of their violation. In them, dignity, gentlemanliness and righteousness coexist with selfishness, viciousness, cruelty and cold-blooded brutality. A worthy person is to be shown all the courtesies and considerations regarded as ideal in human relations, even if a stranger. But a worthless creature, even a close relative like a father or a mother, is killed without the least feeling of guilt. Yet Dinka stories do not have single morals. It is indeed the exception that one moral dominates in a tale. In most cases, various values, sometimes conflicting ones, are advocated. Nor do stories summarize the morals of the tale by way of conclusion. The stories are simply told and left to influence the listeners in a subtle way.

There are several kinds of Dinka folktales. Some concern themselves with the myths of creation and leadership; others deal with certain human faults, such as greed (the tales of Chol Mong from the Rek) and lying (the tales of Ajang Ajiec from the Ngok). Sometimes human characteristics are revealed in animal stories. This tendency is well illustrated by the stories of the Fox and his trickeries. Animal stories also try to explain the distinctive features of animals, their physical appearance, the sounds they make, and their ways of life.

Myths of creation and leadership are historical in nature and purport to be true, although they contain exaggerations and miracles. They are supposed to explain, rationalize, and justify the present. Stories of legendary individuals are of more recent origin and usually concern contemporaries or people only a generation removed. They are also allegedly true, although the individual's prominence provides justification for the continuing invention of stories whose events are then attributed to that individual's life.

The tales in this volume fall into a category which I have called bedtime stories because they are told as people lie in bed ready to sleep. This is not an adequate name, since some stories from the above categories, notably animal stories, are also sometimes told at bedtime. Perhaps the distinguishing characteristic of bedtime stories is that they are not limited to any particular aspect of Dinka life. On the contrary, although individual stories focus on specific issues, bedtime stories as a category cover virtually all aspects of Dinka life and culture.

I have presented the material in three parts. The first introduces the tales by discussing the major characteristics of Dinka folktales and the broad cultural and environmental context in which they operate. The second section contains the translations of the tales. Because bedtime stories concern themselves with the little-known Dinka culture as a whole, in order to make the present collection more meaningful for the reader, in a third part I have tried to provide a comprehensive contextual framework, discussing the content of the tales in terms of relationships to various ideals and practices of Dinka culture and established social processes. Although the Dinka texts are not included in this volume, they are being prepared for a separate publication.

While loyalty to the original material has been a guiding principle in my translation, I have been compelled to substitute some names for the name Deng, which was recurrent with extraordinary frequency. I was asked by almost everyone who read the manuscript to do something about the repetition. Among the names that were originally Deng are Ring in *Aluel and Her Loving Father*, Agany in *Agany and His Search for a Wife*, Teeng in *Diirawic and Her Incestuous Brother*, Kir in *Kir and Ken and Their Addicted Father*, Duang in *Duang and His Wild Wife*, Kon in *Nyanbol and Her Lioness Mother-in-law*, Tuong in *Ajang and His Lioness-Bride*, Kwol in *Achol and Her Adoptive Lioness-Mother*, and Tong in *Ageerpiiu and a Lion*.

The frequency with which the name Deng occurs may be explained in a number of ways, although I must confess that it is for me largely a matter of conjecture. The obvious reason may seem to be that most of the stories were told by relatives. Another reason would seem to be that Deng is a classical name derived from the deity Deng, who is recognized by all Dinka clans. Deng is thus a common name of ancient origin. Its use in tales is not only consistent with this ancient origin, it is also symbolic of the common literary heritage of the Dinka.

The credit for the recording of the folktales goes to a large number of people: relatives, friends, and people I do not know. My brothers Biong and Miokol, and my cousin Kwol Arob, not only tape-recorded the stories, but travelled long distances from one settlement to another in pursuit of stories. While many stories were told especially for them, some were recorded at bedtime under the normal circumstances of storytelling. Sometimes my research assistants were part of the sleeping group, but on occasions they lent their tape recorders to members of the group to capture the normal spirit of storytelling. I am grateful to them and to those who told the stories, and I hope having produced this volume is a sufficient tribute to their efforts.

My gratitude is due to Professor Michael Reisman for kindly undertaking to write the Foreword, and for giving me his time for many enlightening discussions of the tales. My deep appreciation is due Martha Reisman for her inspiring illustrations. Professor Quinton Johnstone read the manuscript and made valuable comments; I am also grateful to him for his long-standing support, encouragement and guidance. Robert Ludwig also read the manuscript and made valuable suggestions for the translation and editing.

A special word of appreciation goes to my dear wife, Dorothy, who not only gave me unfailing encouragement and support, but was a close partner in the translation, the editing, and the general work on the tales.

The material in this volume was partially processed at Yale during the year 1971-72 as part of a wider project supported by a generous grant from the Yale University Program in Law and Modernization. I am most grateful to the Program and to all those individuals whose support was essential.

F.M.D.
*New York,* 1973

# Contents

# Foreword

## Folktales and Civic Acculturation: Reflections on the Myths of Dinkaland

*Michael Reisman*

Because the tales of the Dinka which Dr. Deng has here collected are so beautiful, their value as world art may overshadow their significance as devices of socialization and civic acculturation in traditional society.* All folktales contain a residuum of group experience whose intergenerational transmission is assured by the very recounting of the tales. Cultures as well as civilizations must find ways of instilling components of the social code which are not appropriate for direct discourse. Often a way must be found to provide dramatic illustrations of how people balance the "do's" and "don't's" of group life in those dynamic situations which seem so much more complicated than the normative code. Stories can be a particularly useful social carrier, particularly where the audiences are culturally unfamiliar with the processes of transforming normative formulations into casuistic applications or are distrustful of the authority source from which direct communication of information might come. In the United States, for

---

* Acculturation is, of course, only one function of the tales, as Edwin Smith has suggested: "The Function of Folk Tales", *Journal of the Royal African Society*, Vol. 39, 1940, pp. 64-83. Any cultural practice performs multiple social functions, latent and manifest. The functions need not be entirely compatible, nor need they all be socially useful. Some may impede physical health or neurological organization. Other functions may generate unwanted conflict, for example, wars which increase the probability of extermination of the culture. Thus, the Jibaro Indians seem to recognize that intertribal war and intratribal blood feuds are the most fundamental practice of their culture and yet one which seems certain to lead to their extinction. Karsten, "Blood Revenge and War Among the Jibaro Indians of Eastern Ecuador," in Bohannan, *War and Warfare: Studies in the Anthropology of Conflict*, p. 304 (1967).

example, efforts at disseminating welfare and health information have often met with little success, while incorporating the same information into the plot of a drama or even daily television soap opera seems to have transmitted the information and inspired people to act upon it.

In any culture, all non-linear and non-textual communication devices may be used to convey basic code information; in a folk culture, these devices are, perforce, the primary media. Conversely, as functional anthropology has shown, in the aggregate of a culture's manifest and latent communications one finds the code and its supporting social calculus. Within this aggregate, the folktale is not the exclusive nor necessarily the most effective acculturative device. And yet the folktale in traditional societies does have a distinctive, added dimension. It can "create" personal decision experiences for listeners, with an artful suspense which almost magically involves the listener. He catches his breath and his heart beats rapidly because, for a moment, the folktale's social choices with all their glowing or dire consequences almost seem to be his.

If folktales are to be effective as instruments of socialization and civic acculturation, there must be recurring and perhaps even institutionalized situations for their transmission. In many circumstances, the transmission is to children and is performed by nursemaids or women in domestic situations. But ethnographers have also observed certain material and social structures which conduce to the generation and recitation of tales. Quiet group work—for example, grafting in vineyards—is an inviting situation for a storyteller, who can entertain his co-workers and make time move more easily without hindering the work. Field houses or guild hostels in which people gather after work and before sleep have been another important folktale arena.* And, of course, it is not unlikely that a culture in which tales are a critical strut may establish occupational and recreational situations facilitating tale recitation.

---

* It is as yet unclear what the intervening effect of communications technology, particularly the transistor, will be on patterns of traditional acculturation. I would hypothesize that the effectiveness of technological intervention in traditional societies and folk-culture strata of civilizations will be directly proportional to the degree to which the external communicator builds on and operates within the phenomenal world of his audience: conforming to the matter-of-fact expectations of the past and the future of his audience, being consonant with audience demands and activating a positive rather than negative identification with the audience.

Folktale recitation is highly institutionalized among the Dinka; hence the acculturative potentialities of the tales are enormously enhanced. The stories are told, in bantering exchanges, as a family of several generations prepares to go to sleep in a hut or a byre.* In the relief of the evening, in the mysterious light of day-night, in the unique state of pre-sleep, all listeners are probably more receptive to suggestion than they would be at other times during the day. At these moments, the tales can convey many facets of Dinka experience which may be only implicit in language and behavior, and may not be stated at other times or in other forms. Yet a knowledge of these experiences may be indispensable for performing civic roles in Dinka life. Viewed from this perspective, Dr. Deng's collection of tales provides us with stunning insights into aspects of Dinka life and social regulation which are at once different and exotic and yet easily recognizable as strains in the universal repertory of human experience.

Many of the stories explore, instruct and exemplify incest prohibitions and other social limits of sexual affection between and within generations by tracing the incest theme through several generations and families, managing to convey tabooed passions with clarity and yet with delicacy, subtlety and some sympathy. Sexual attraction, cohesive as well as divisive, cannot be biologically limited; hence a fundamental artifact of any social organization is acculturation to legitimate targets of affection and the establishment and inculcation of a code of appropriate quanta and forms of affective expression. In some cases, as Professor Goode argues, acculturated controls may seek to check the disruptive effect of love on stratification and lineage patterns. In other cases, the controls may respond to psychological needs.

---

* There are some striking cross-cultural parallels in formulae initiating the recitation of tales. Compare, for example, Dr. Deng's description of the Dinka formulation in his Introduction with the information of József Faragó about the timbermen of Marosmagyaró, Hungary:

> The tale runs on, time passes. Some become tired and fall asleep. The storyteller at some moment says "bones," to which the answer has to be "soup," as a sign that one is not falling asleep but is listening. Some who have already fallen asleep instinctively answer drowsily, but belatedly and very slowly. This causes loud laughter. Gradually, everyone gets tired and finally falls asleep. The question "bones" is answered by "soup" by fewer and fewer people, sounds lower and lower, and finally the storyteller lets be. (From Linda Dégh, *Folktales and Society: Storytelling in a Hungarian Peasant Community*, p. 84, Indiana University Press, 1969.)

While "Oedipus" may be a fundamental constitutive psychological experience, the code of any culture must deal with many relationships beside that of mother-son. What is appropriate for each relationship may vary with respect to target, ritual, time, place, quantum and intensity of affection. The complex code for all of these relationships is established and transmitted in diverse situations and in many different formulated and unformulated communications. In another dimension, the "structure" of the tale or the residual group experiences frozen in the language may itself influence the content of the code. Sometimes social structure itself—for example, the nuclear family—may imply, contain, or facilitate the application of the code.* Among the Dinka, the extended family and polygamy provide fertile soil for intergenerational sexual conflict. The strong attraction between the new young wife of an elder Dinka and his adult son can become malignant family tension because both father and son know that the son will inherit this wife upon the elder's death. It is common for sexual mastery to be intertwined with prestige, social respect and location in a power structure. Among the Dinka, these problems are sometimes discussed openly between father and son, apparently on the basis of certain shared norms of a code earlier acquired, perhaps through tales.

Consider the story *Aluel and Her Loving Father*. When his beautiful young bride died in childbirth, Chol shifted his love to his daughter, Aluel. Ordinarily her mother's family would have raised her, but Chol insisted on doing it himself, performing all the maternal tasks which the Dinka consider inappropriate for the father. As Aluel grew, she sensed the incongruity and insisted that her father remarry. Chol's second wife was jealous of her husband's love for Aluel; she deprived her stepdaughter of food and even named her own daughter Aluel. Just as Aluel had sensed the pathological dimensions of her father's love and had sought to deflect it to a new wife, the second Aluel grasped the excessive jealousy of her natural mother and attempted to curb it. Both daughters failed, but each remained loyal to her erring parent.

Aluel had persuaded her father to visit her maternal relatives and to redeem his bridewealth. But then Aluel was despondent and longed for Chol. Her stepmother exploited his absence to drive Aluel from the village

---

* It may provide a setting which generates precisely those conflicts which the code anticipates.

to search for her father, supposedly hiding behind the Sun. Struck by the Sun, Aluel chased it until the Sun took her home to his own two barren wives, who raised her as their common daughter. Even here the wives' affection took perverted forms of jealousy and competition over the girl.

Meanwhile, Chol returned to find his daughter gone. Insane with grief, he was chained in a cattle-byre where he mourned for years. The Sun, witnessing his anguish day after day, finally concluded that Chol would die if Aluel were not returned. When Chol was told of the impending return of his daughter, he prepared for her quite furtively; the villagers never suspected that the conclusion of this epic period of mourning was due to Aluel's return. Even the reason for Chol's ecstatic sacrifice of bulls, goats, and rams was concealed from the villagers. Aluel had returned, and Chol would have her to himself.

But in another village, a young man named Ring, gifted with mystical abilities, saw the entire sequence of events and determined that Aluel would be his bride. He reached Chol's village, overcame Chol's dissimulations and betrothed Aluel. With the help of all the villagers, Ring succeeded in persuading Chol to allow them to leave for his own village. When Aluel left, Chol killed his second wife.

The same theme is now inverted in a new setting. At his own village, Ring is prevented from consummating his marriage by his father, who has become infatuated with Aluel and insists upon her for himself. The father challenges his son to fight for the girl. But this is tantamount to Ring's suicide, for only the father has cattle, and one cannot engage in a spear duel without a hide-shield. Ring's father plays craftily on Ring's affections by suggesting that the son kill his mother and make a shield out of her skin, thus sharpening the conflict between affective lines and reinforcing generational authority. Ring is, of course, unwilling to do this and prepares to surrender Aluel to his father. But Ring's mother intervenes and insists that Ring slaughter and skin her in order to fight his father for Aluel. Only half her skin is to be used for the shield. The other half, she insists, must be set aside and used for Ring's marriage bed should he win the duel.

Ring slays his mother, fashions a shield from her skin and goes to meet his father. Ring's twin brothers, Ngor and Chan, crouch behind each contestant, exhorting each to miss the target every time a spear is hurled. This goes on for several days, until one of the twins becomes impatient and tells Ring to hit his father. Ring spears him fatally, and as the father dies, he surrenders Aluel to his son, explaining that it was impossible to relinquish the girl as long as he lived. Thereafter Aluel mourns her mother-in-law constantly, but the couple produces enough children to found a nation.

The conclusion of the Aluel story transforms it into a nation-myth, more complex yet parallel to the myths of Darwin and Freud concerning the primal horde. But there is no sense of guilt or implied admonition, such as one finds in Freud's reconstruction of the primal-horde myth. The fantasies of violence against the older generation, which actually has authority and effective power, can be a rich artistic device for a multi-generational audience.* Yet the outcome of the violence is deemed just, and the tale itself conveys a complex of norms and their dramatic social sanctions. In the same manner, in the tale of *Deng and His Vicious Step-mother*, a mother's illicit passion for her stepson is punished by her natural son, who kills her, her brother and his son; the narrator conveys no moral disapprobation of these acts. In each case, violence, though tragic, has been used to punish those who violated the code, and the effect is to reinforce notions of appropriate behavior in affection. Similarly, in *Nyanbol and Her Lioness Mother-in-law*, the mother who devours all her son's brides is finally recognized as a lioness and burned to death in her hut. *Deng and His Vicious Stepmother* uses some extraordinary artistic devices. The powerful erotic undertone of the story is controlled by depicting the sexual act initiated by the stepmother as a partial castration and by emphasizing repeatedly the stepmother's non-consanguineous relation to her stepson. A further refinement which seems to be characteristic of Dinka tales is the transformation of a human being into an animal (and in certain cases, into a foreigner) when that human is about to commit a socially reprehensible act.†

* The obverse of this device is the explicit, dramatized treatment of the sexual attraction of the parents toward the mates of their children. Note that Ring's mother, in contrast to his father, can be a prominent participant in the consummation of her son's marriage, but her highly erotic role is licit because it facilitates the marriage.

† Transformations into different animals constitute very complex symbols in these tales; unfortunately, there is insufficient material here for explication. As in European folktales, human beings can be transformed into other species, for example, hyenas, and it may be that different species emphasize different qualities. In Dr. Deng's collection of tales the lion-man or woman often expresses a sexuality whose vigor breaches the social code. Yet

In *Diirawic and Her Incestuous Brother* many of the same artistic devices are used to portray the establishment of the sibling incest taboo in Dinka culture. The brother of the beautiful Diirawic has become infatuated with his sister and marries her. Diirawic protects herself by castrating and killing the brother on the wedding night. Then she and all the young women of her age-set flee to the forest. There a lion which tries to devour Diirawic is tricked by the girls, beaten and ritually transformed into a human being. The former lion is accepted as Diirawic's brother and returns with the girls to the village. Diirawic marries another man, the lion marries other women, and all live in harmony. When Diirawic's thirteenth child proves to be a lion, i.e., wild and sexually aggressive, the lion-brother kills the child. This myth establishes, with extraordinary power, the Dinka's perceived need for strict boundaries regarding type and intensity of affection between brother and sister to maintain social order.

The theme of incest and intergenerational competition is treated more daringly in *Chol and His Baby-Bride*, for in this tale there is a subtle hint that society began by a violation of incest prohibitions. The very young wife of an elderly man was barren until the husband atoned for marrying her before puberty by the sacrifice of *agorot*. When she conceived and gave birth to a girl, a young man named Chol insisted on attending the infant and raising her himself. Before her puberty, Chol, now a much older man, betrothed the girl he had raised, but before marriage, the girl was stolen by a lioness who had become infatuated with her. Chol rescues the girl, slays the lion and secures its blessing. They are married and produce enough children for a nation.

Dr. Deng's collection of stories indicates that the Dinka tales are not only concerned with inculcating the fundamental sexual taboos of society. Many other values are transmitted. For instance, a number of the stories deal dramatically with the pervasive human problem of balancing appetite and social obligation: the management or economy of the libido. As in most traditional societies, the complex filagree of customary privileges and obligations with different kin groups is the very bedrock of social organi-

---

in the more general Dinka cosmology, the lion is not the goat; indeed, it may be a totem. It is also worth noting that the Dinka cosmology does not rely on the hierarchical conception found, for example, in the Genesis myth. It is a coarchical system in which all species coexist, often by alliance and treaty.

zation; loyalties are the cement of social order. But the Dinka are not puritans; they enjoy their senses. Hence they establish and inculcate a code that balances self-indulgence and self-repression. Indeed, self-sufficiency and self-restraint are considered *dheeng* or correct, cultured, even noble comportment. The appropriate ways of applying these principles in dynamic contexts is given in the tales. Thus, the mother who was so foolishly lazy that she would trade a limb for a moment's aid in performing a trivial, mundane chore loses her arms and legs and becomes an animal. She is transformed into a human being by being roundly beaten by her children.* In another tale, the father of Kir and Ken is so addicted to tobacco that he is about to sell his children in order to get a supply. Fortunately, Kir and Ken seize enough tobacco for their father. But the father, by his self-indulgence and disloyalty to his sons, forfeits his share of family wealth; when he still insists on it, the sons kill him. In *Duang and His Wild Wife*, the problem of self-regulating personal appetite, loyalty and social obligation is most refined. Amou's gluttonous compulsion to eat meat finally alienates her husband, and he gives her dog meat instead of beef. Poisoned, she becomes a wild lion. Her children remain loyal to her, however, and after a period of confusion, they catch her and beat her, and through this ritual bring her back to humanity. Amou's husband is quite happy to receive her now that she is cured of her compulsion, but Amou desires revenge and, with ironic justice, kills her husband by feeding him to death. In each of these tales, the tension and anxiety over being abandoned by kin with a duty of care is resolved by socially approved violence against the relative who breached the code, reassuring potential dependents, deterring potential principals and cementing the bonds of kinship.†

Tales such as these establish and reinforce, for each generation, the fundamentals of the social code deemed necessary for group life. As an instrument for civic acculturation, the folktale has a unique impact. It creates artistically an imaginary situation in which a critical decision must be made and then judges the decision. If the art is effective, those who hear

---

* The ritual beating in several of the stories must have a particular charm for the children who listen to the stories, for it often turns a fundamental sanction used by their elders against the elders themselves.
† In this Dinka tales may be compared with certain Mediterranean folktales in which precisely the opposite social ethic is acculturated. An extraordinary African contrast may be found in Neil Skinner (ed.), *Hausa Tales and Traditions* (1970).

the tale almost live the decision. Hence the tales are a decisive education for the young because they are entertaining, dramatic and artistically satisfying. As Dr. Deng's studies of the tales show, they are more than simple organic growths; in part, they are changed and manipulated to secure certain ends. This suggests that the structures of folk society are as malleable, within their social context, as those of civilizations, that civic acculturation there is not substantially different from the regulated and often institutionalized acculturation in our own societies. And the range of participation may be significantly higher. The Dinka tales are "traded" each evening by most of the participants, and in contrast to what prevails in many other folk societies, the membrane between teller and audience is highly permeable; the constant fashioning of the group's future by a reworking of its past becomes a shared process. Whatever the formal authority structure of the group may be, the tale process can provide a measure of democracy in the prescription and termination of norms of the social code. Because of the inexorable specialization of functions in civilizations, wide participation in the shaping of group futures through social prescription can be achieved, if at all, only by careful structuring of the legal and political processes of authoritative and effective power. In many parts of the world, political structures of wide participation have not, unfortunately, proved particularly durable. Perhaps some form of contemporary folktale, like that of the Dinka, might be revived as a conscious contemporary political technique.

# INTRODUCTION

IN this introduction, I limit my comments to three major characteristics of Dinka tales: their fusion of fantasy and reality, their original and contemporary relevance, and the circumstances under which they are told. I later analyze the contents of the tales in relation to various aspects of the Dinka social process.

## FANTASY AND REALITY

In folktales the Dinka construct a world of cosmic totality in which human beings, animals, trees and spirits not only interact, but can also change their forms or perform deeds unnatural to their species. The two main categories governing this world are those of human and non-human behavior. The focus tends to be on human interaction with lions, perhaps because lions are what the Dinka fear the most. In Ngok Dinka dialect, bedtime stories are called *koor*, i.e., "lions," and lions appear very frequently in them. But the idea is more far-reaching and permits anything to change into anything else. As a Dinka once said about a bedtime story in which such objects as stones, grass, straws, and rafters spoke: "The Dinka want to show that everything has breath and feels pain; everything deserves to be treated like a human being." As I later argue, the conceptualization of story-participants as lions would seem to suggest more than cosmic totality. It is also a moral classification based on adherence to and violation of the fundamental precepts of the Dinka code. Nonetheless, a moral classification set up in these terms is made possible by the fact that the Dinka live in an environment in which human beings coexist, interact, harmonize and clash with animals and other elements of nature.

Animals as ferocious as the lion are sometimes consecrated as totems of clans; they are thereby affiliated as "relatives" and must not be killed by members of their clan. This is understandable in the case of such beautiful animals as the giraffe, which, despite its delicious meat, is allowed to roam in the villages of its "relatives" without being hurt. But almost every animal has some clan which "respects" it and "honors" its relationship to that clan.

Affiliation with non-human elements goes beyond animals and covers almost all things: rivers, fish, snakes, trees, grass, even disease. A relationship may dictate that people not fish in certain rivers, that certain fish not be caught, that certain snakes not be killed, that certain trees not be felled, that the wood of certain trees not be burnt, that certain grass not be cut, that certain diseases be treated only by certain clans, and the like. Even when an animal may be eaten, certain parts must not be roasted but boiled, certain bones must not be broken, and certain meat must not be eaten by certain persons. Violating any of these norms may bring a curse which may end in a calamity. All totems require sacrifice or dedication of livestock on regular bases or whenever their help is specifically needed. Generally, they are expected to protect their human relatives from the malevolent forces of illness and death or from any other mishap. But if not appropriately treated, they may themselves be a source of evil and destruction.

Animals and other creatures tend to feel safe with the people who consider them relatives and in return do not harm them. Lions and crocodiles have been said to go to the homes of their relatives to eat animals given to them. They would eat and leave without hurting anyone. As dangerous snakes as the puff-adder may be patted on the back by a relative, given butter to lick, and then carefully taken away, assured that this is not a rejection but a way to safety, so that human beings or animals will not trample over them and hurt them accidentally. Such snakes have been known to sleep in the same bed with people, even rest their heads on human beings, and not harm them. When they harm their relatives, it is said to be because of some wrong committed by the relatives they harm or by someone closely related to them. In view of the close inter-dependencies between relatives, vicarious responsibility is a striking feature of Dinka law. Even when dead, the spirit of a wronged snake may haunt the living relatives and take vengeance.

The Dinka world of fantasy goes beyond what I have just presented. The Dinka believe that the sun travels from the East to the West. At night, it returns from the West to the East to be ready to rise again. Man should not see the sun on its return journey. Seeing it return, which some people claim to do, is a spiritual intrusion which is likely to be punished unless remedied by appropriate rites of atonement. Thunder is seen as the voice of God angered by the evils of man. Lightning is the club by which God strikes at the evils of man, and even when it kills, the submissive response of the Dinka is, "Our Father has seen; the right is on His side." And God receives more dedications and sacrifices.

Dinka concepts of illness and well-being embody a great deal of magico-religious philosophy which transcends that reality which even the Dinka recognize as the normal. "Black Magicians" can victimize even innocent people through symbolic action based on the premise that what is wished is achieved. Benevolent magicians remove evil spells with the same principle. A black magician can blind his victim, cast snakes into his stomach, and perhaps mortally pierce his heart. A benevolent magician can open the eyes, remove the snakes, and perhaps save a pierced heart. All this the Dinka accept without being literal about the meaning of truth. Indeed, they are well aware of the fact that the truth of magic is something other than the ordinary truth.

While the fantasy of Dinka folktales can be objectively related to the supernatural phenomena of Dinka life, the Dinka would be more likely to see fantasy in mythical terms that attribute the cosmic interaction to an original state of affairs which no longer exists. In the beginning, according to Dinka myth, God was linked with the world, and all things then interacted in an atmosphere of perfection. Everything was the ultimate of goodness. Then man, or actually, woman, committed an offense which provoked God into withdrawing from the world and willing that man should strive, suffer, and die. The world envisioned by folktales is closely analogous to the original world of cosmic interaction, though it is far from being a world of perfect harmony and happiness. In the world of Dinka tales, there is *real* suffering and death. The stories try to weld together the myth of a once-united world and the realities of a disrupted world. Their inconsistency is part of their basic logic and does not bother the Dinka. In their folktales, the Dinka do not, of course, mean to tell the real truth. They do not speak of "telling" a story but of *paar*, a difficult word to translate; it is close to guessing but implies an attempt to reconstruct as much of the truth as possible from the scanty information available.

Fantasy permits the Dinka to see the presence and absence of values in extreme terms. A hero is the most handsome, the strongest, the fastest, the kindest, and the most virtuous. A heroine is the most beautiful and the most virtuous person there ever was. Sometimes the evil ones are also endowed with some extreme virtues that enable them to attain their goals. Thus it is the most beautiful lion-girl who seduces and victimizes the hero, and it is the most handsome lion who captures the heroine. But, while most tales end in a great deal of destruction to life and property, "the bad guys" eventually lose and "the good guys" win. A hero or a heroine who has been killed is recreated with superior attributes; if ill-treated or otherwise deprived, he or she is compensated and indulged to the opposite extreme.

This combination of the extreme negative realities of life with a vision of the extreme positives that proper conduct wins is an important element in the dreams that are so vital for motivation towards the goals which society sets for its members, particularly its children.

## ORIGIN AND RELEVANCE

A significant element in the fusion of fantasy and reality is the attribution of an ancient origin to folktales. Dinka folktales are supposed to begin and, in fact, mostly begin with "this is an ancient event." Yet they not only reflect the sum-total of Dinka culture, but also mention specific current facts. For instance, age-sets, which are functional generational units that every Dinka joins on attaining majority, are designated in the stories by the names of contemporary age-sets and are also identified with living individuals as the age-sets of so-and-so. This way, what is attributed to the past in the tales is made relevant to the present, and is thus more easily conceptualized and better understood.

But the significance of the present in Dinka folktales is more than a conceptual convenience in communication. Novelties are incorporated into a cultural experience which is allegedly ancient and is considered part of the over-all heritage of the Dinka. Governments, guns, police, lawful executions, and horses are included in folktales despite the fact that they are of recent origin in Dinka experience.

It is because folktales allow for a great deal of creativity that some people are better storytellers than others. A good storyteller may make a good story out of a bad one and a bad storyteller may spoil a good one. It is not unusual to find that the same stories told by different people will differ in matters of detail, or will remain the same to a certain stage, after which they diverge.

In some instances, the details which account for the differences reflect the status of the storytellers. If the storyteller comes from a large family, success in the end may lead to the hero's marrying a large number of wives, then living with them in much the same way as the family of the storyteller lives.

## CIRCUMSTANCES OF DELIVERY

The fantasies of folktales, their mysterious origin, and their relevance to real life puts them in a dreamy domain which the Dinka recognize by the circumstances under which stories are told. Stories should not be told during the daytime, but at bedtime, as a prelude to going to sleep. In fact, they often function as lullabies not only for children but also for adults. Usually the sleeping company is mixed; adults and children sleep together in huts. Most storytelling groups are made up of women and children, although men may share a sleeping-place with older boys and tell stories. There is a close association between storytelling and the presence of children, but adults are not only the main source of stories, they also enjoy telling and hearing them.

When people have gone to bed, one person, usually a good storyteller, is asked to tell a story. Sometimes she or he will insist on knowing who will "pay the reverse bridewealth," who will tell the next story. Reverse bridewealth is the payment the relatives of a girl make to the bridegroom, who pays the main bridewealth for his wife. Usually reverse payment is about one-third of what a man pays for a girl, but it must be paid by her relatives from their own cattle, not from the cattle paid them by the bridegroom. The significance of its use in the context of storytelling is rather obscure, although it does indicate the family orientation and the cattle complex of the Dinka. In any event, there is nearly always someone willing to tell another story after a story has been told. So one after another tells stories.

As the storytelling progresses, people begin to fall asleep one by one.

Sometimes they fall asleep, wake up in the middle of a story, and then fall asleep again. This is possible because some stories tend to be rather long. People who wake up in the middle of a story are usually brought up to date briefly. As time passes and some people begin to sleep and perhaps snore, the storyteller starts to ask from time to time, "Are you asleep?" This is an amusing stage; people keep drifting back into sleep or drowsily struggle to remain awake. As long as there are people still awake, storytelling continues. The last storyteller is quite likely to be the last person awake, and so the final story will be left incomplete. But there may be someone else awake for whom the story will be completed; then an agreement may be reached on going to sleep so that no more stories will be told for the night.

The darkness of the night in which stories are told provides a setting which facilitates the fusing fantasy in the stories. After all, the usual animal of the stories—the lion—is often heard roaring at night even as the stories are told. The mysteriousness of the night and the circumstances of delivery give stories a quality which approximates a dream. Furthermore, they in fact make people sleep, and so form a bridge between reality and dream world.

# THE TALES

# Aluel and Her Loving Father

THIS IS AN ANCIENT EVENT.

Ayak was so beautiful! A man called Chol married her. She went to her home and conceived while still a new bride. She spent months pregnant. Then she gave birth to a girl. The day she gave birth, she suddenly died. When her husband saw that, he took the baby and put her on his lap while she was still that small. People tried to stop him, saying, "How can you hold such a newborn baby? Let someone else hold her."

But he refused, saying, "I cannot allow this child to be held by someone else. I will hold her myself. By killing her mother, God willed that I should suffer." So she was left to him to hold and take care of. They stayed inside the cattle-byre. He named her Aluel and raised her all by himself. His wife had left everything in the house. There was plenty of grain. One day, women from a nearby village came and said, "Why don't you give us some grain so that we may prepare food for you?" But he refused, saying, "I don't want to eat."

So he stayed like that, drinking only milk and feeding his daughter only milk too. He raised her until she grew up. First she crawled, then she walked, and then she became a big girl. Even as a little girl, she was good with words. When she grew big, she became very well-spoken.

One day, she called her father. And as they sat together, she said to him, "Father!"

"Yes, my daughter," answered her father.

"Now that you stay alone without marrying," she continued, "am I to remain forever without a brother or sister?"

33

Her father was surprised by her question. "Daughter," he said, "how did you think of this?"

"If you had married," she explained, "I would perhaps have had a brother or a sister and my stepmother might have been like a mother to me."

"My daughter!" he said.

"Yes, Father!" she replied.

"What prevents me from marrying is fear of the usual ways of step-mothers. If I married, my wife might treat you like an orphan. She might even influence me to the point where I might forget you."

"Never," she said. "What you are saying is not so. If she should come and ill-treat me, then you and I will see to that when it happens. But that you should remain alone is not right."

They talked and talked about the matter for months, until her father agreed. Then he married and brought his wife home. He seated her near him and said to her, "You see this child of mine. I stayed for all this time unmarried because I did not want to marry, I wanted to remain with her and her mother. I wanted to live with her and remember her mother through her. I never even thought I would ever marry again. But when my daughter thought and spoke of such a big subject when she was only a child, I honored her words and married you. So if you mistreat her in any way, know that we will not share this home with you." That was how he talked to his wife.

At first, the woman treated the child well. But then she began to behave in her own way. As she milked for the girl, she would first pour water into the milk gourd and then put milk on top of the water. When the little girl tried to drink her milk, she found it watery. So she would turn the milk gourd upside down and spill the milk without being seen by her stepmother. Sometimes her stepmother would not even give her a share of the food she cooked.

Whenever the girl went to her father, he would notice her condition and say, "My child, why is your stomach like that? Are you hungry?"

She would answer, "No, Father, I am not hungry, I have eaten."

Her father would argue, "My child, you have not eaten. If you had eaten, you would not be like this!"

The girl would insist and even swear: "May I die, by God, Father, I have eaten."

Her father would ignore her words and say, "Have this food and eat."

"No, Father, I cannot eat again," she would continue to say.

Her father would persuade her at least to drink some milk. That she would eventually do.

That was the way they lived. Her stepmother continued to behave in the same way and her father continued to question her and offer her food and milk. She would refuse the food and drink the milk. This happened almost every day.

Her stepmother gave birth to a daughter, who was also named Aluel. To distinguish her from her older sister, she was called "the younger Aluel." Her older sister then became known as "the older Aluel." The woman took good care of her own daughter, but continued to ill-treat her stepchild.

When her own child grew up to understand things and speak well, she noticed what her mother was doing to her half sister. One day, she spoke to her mother: "Mother!"

"Yes!" answered her mother.

"Why do you ill-treat my sister, Aluel? You do not give her food and her milk is always watery and not like mine. Why do you behave like that? Don't you see that she is my sister? Is she not as though she were my mother's own child? Is her being without a mother not enough to make you treat her like your own child?"

"My daughter," replied her mother, "how do I ill-treat her? What sort of a daughter are you anyway? What do you want to do to me? I suppose you plan to go and tell your father that Aluel is badly treated!"

"No," her daughter assured her, "I will not tell anyone."

Her daughter complained to her mother many times about the way she was treating her half sister, but she never reported her to her father.

One day, the older Aluel went to her father and said: "Father!"

"Yes, my daughter."

"Here you are staying only in one place. You have never even visited my mother's relatives since my mother died. You remember my mother's mother wanted to take care of me in her house and you refused. All this time, you have suffered much taking care of me all by yourself without any help from them. You have not been able to collect from my mother's relatives the cattle of reverse bridewealth.* Even the cattle to which you are entitled from the marriages of my mother's sisters and cousins, you have never gone to claim from my maternal relatives.† Don't you think it would be better if you visited them to see whether you could come back with some cattle to increase our herd?"

"Daughter," said her father, "my heart is afraid. You are right, ever since you were born, I have never gone away from here. Even a place as near as that village, I have never visited. And it is because of you that my heart fears. If I were to leave, who knows what might befall you in my absence!"

"Nothing will happen to me," said his daughter. "You should go."

"Never!" persisted her father.

For nearly a month, they discussed the matter. Eventually, her father agreed to go. When the time came for him to actually leave, he would start and return from a short distance to repeat his words to his wife: "I am leaving my daughter with you. If you should mistreat her in my absence, we will not live together in this house."

The woman responded, saying, "How can I mistreat her? Is it because you are going to be away that you think I might change and treat her badly when I have never treated her badly?"

"When I leave," he said, "the heart of a stepmother may make you do something harmful to her."

She acted quite offended and said, "It is really insulting for you to doubt me this way. How can I act jealously when her mother is not living? If she were living, you might have been right. Nothing will happen to her."

Aluel never told her father how her stepmother treated her. Her father had doubts because of what he saw and not because of anything she said. So he believed his wife's words and left.

He went and stayed away for some time. Aluel missed her father very much. She would sit and cry. One day, her stepmother thought of playing a trick on her. The sun had turned red as it was setting. She called the girl and pointed at the setting sun, saying, "You see that man near the sun? It

* Among the Dinka, it is the man and his relatives who pay bridewealth for the wife, but the relatives of the bride are expected to pay from their own cattle an amount equivalent to one-third of the bridewealth to assist the newlyweds in establishing themselves.
† Depending on his wife's order of birth in relation to her sisters, a man is entitled to share in the bridewealth of some of his sisters-in-law

is your father. I saw him come and suddenly, he turned to follow the sun. I can't understand what has happened to him. You better run after him and find out!"

"Really?" the girl said with excitement, and she started running towards the setting sun. She ran and ran until she realized that she did not see anybody where she was going. So she returned and said, "Mother, I do not see my father. I don't think he is there."

"Is that why you returned?" asked her stepmother. "Of course it is your father. What a fool you are! I don't think you really want your father! How could you come back and leave him?"

The girl cried and started running again. She ran and ran and never returned. She went as far as the big river which the Sun was crossing. She arrived at the river as the Sun fell into the water. When she got into the river, she found that the water had been heated by the Sun so much that her body nearly blistered. When the Sun had crossed to the other side of the river, he extended his arm back to her and pulled her out of the water onto the other side. Then he spoke to her. "Where have you come from?"

"It was my stepmother who made me leave our home!" she answered.

"She did?" said the Sun with sympathy.

"Yes, she did!" replied Aluel.

"What about your mother? Was she there, or don't you have a mother?"

"I have no mother," she answered.

"Well, never mind," said the Sun. "Come, let us go home."

So they left. The Sun held her hand as they walked.

The Sun had two wives at home. Of course, the wives of the Sun do not bear children.* They were both barren.† When the Sun brought the girl home, they were exceedingly glad. Each one shouted her claim, "She is mine! She will live with me!"

But the Sun said, "This child will live with both of you. Each one of

* At first I thought the use of the phrase "of course" did not make sense. Consequently I omitted it and translated the sentence as "Neither of them had given birth." This degree of distortion troubled me. I kept wondering what "of course" could signify in the context of general usage. One day about a year later, it suddenly occurred to me that if the Sun could have children, there would be many suns. Since there continues to be only one Sun, it must mean that the Sun does not reproduce.

† Although it is reasonable to assume that the Sun's childlessness is more likely to be due to his sterility than to the barrenness of all the women he marries, the Dinka are more prone to attribute childlessness to barrenness than to sterility.

you must look after her well. If you do not treat her well, that will be bad and I will quarrel with you. Most likely, her father is now suffering very much."

"Very well," said the women.

They both took good care of her. One would give her food and gifts today and the other would do the same the following day. They would bathe her, anoint her body, and do all sorts of things for her comfort and pleasure. Although she was a big girl, each of the wives would call her, seat her on her lap, and ask her: "Aluel, which of us two do you love the most?"

She would answer, "O, which of you can I say I love more? Are you both not my mothers?"

They would pursue their questions: "How can two be equally lovable mothers to the point where the child does not feel some preference in her heart?"

But she remained firm. "I love you both equally."

They each continued putting her to the test, but she always responded the same way: "You are exactly the same to me. Neither of you is better than the other." So they stayed and she grew up among them to be a mature girl.

In the meantime, her father returned home. As soon as he arrived on the edge of the village, he asked, "Where has Aluel gone? Why does she not come to meet me?"

Her stepmother explained, "Aluel left a few days ago. She suddenly started to run, saying that she saw a man whom she wanted to meet. So she ran after that man and never returned. I tried to stop her, but she could not be stopped. Since then, I have been searching for her but have not been able to find her."

Her father suddenly became frantic. "Is that not what I feared? Is that not what I warned my daughter about?" He started shouting wildly.

So he was caught and chained. He stayed chained and refused to eat. Even milk he would not drink. He only drank water. He stayed that way, all alone, chained in the cattle-byre, shouting all night and shouting all day.

As the Sun went overhead to his home in the West, he saw him in that condition; and when he returned at night from the West to his home in the East, he also found him crying in the same way.

The girl grew big until she became a mature girl. The Sun decorated her with bracelets and put ivory bangles on her arms. And they stayed together.

One day the Sun called his wives and told them: "I think this girl must go."

As soon as he started to say that, his wives began to cry. "Where is she to go?" they asked.

"Her father is suffering very much," he explained to them. "Every time I pass above him, I find him crying. For the years this girl has been with us, never once have I found him in peace. So I think we should return her to him. He is really suffering. The girl was an orphan whose mother died and he alone brought her up. If she stays away from him, he will probably die. At present, he is mad."

His wives cried: "This cannot be!"

But the Sun insisted. That night, the Sun left on his way to the East. He stopped on top of the cattle-byre. He found the man crying as usual and called to him, "Man in the cattle-byre!"

The man listened.

Again he shouted, "Man in the cattle-byre!"

Then the man responded, "Yes!"

"Please listen to my words very carefully," the Sun said. "I am on my way. I am late and I am afraid the morning may find me before I return home."

"Who are you?" asked the man. "Who is speaking to me?"

"It is I, the Sun."

"What do you want from me? What are you saying? Have you never come across such a miserable person?"

"I have seen your misery," said the Sun. "All these years, I have passed over you and seen you crying. I know why you cry. Your daughter is alive; she is with me."

As soon as he heard that, Aluel's father began to cry again. Then he fainted.

"Please listen to my words," said the Sun. "I must go! I am very late! Within two or three days, make some poles. Make them long enough to reach the roof of your cattle-byre. Bring them inside the byre and make a platform on them. In two or three days, I will bring your daughter and place her there."

When Chol heard what the Sun was saying, he fainted.

The Sun said, "I am now on my way. You better do these things."

Chol remained. Early the next morning, he said to the people, "Please give me milk!"

He was given milk.

Then he said, "Please prepare some food for me!"

Food was prepared for him.

Then he said, "Please unchain me."

He was unchained. He could not walk. It was as though he were crippled. He limped to the forest and cut down some trees for the poles. Then he returned.

People wondered, "What has the old man, Chol, thought of today?"

Some people said, "O people, is it not that he has given up? It has been a very long time. No one has ever mourned for so long. He has abandoned all hope; he knows she cannot return."

Many people agreed, "Yes, he must have given up."

All agreed that he behaved that way because he had lost all hope. He came and put up his poles in the cattle-byre and made his platform.

After three days, the Sun took the child with him. The wives of the Sun suffered so much from the idea of the girl leaving them that it caused trouble in the Sun's household. But the Sun felt that he should take the child. And so he did.

He arrived with the girl at the man's home early in the morning. "Are you in the cattle-byre?" the Sun asked.

"Yes," answered Chol.

"Here, take your daughter!"

As the Sun spoke, Chol fainted.

"You are only delaying me," said the Sun. "Don't you see I am behind time? Receive your daughter!"

He became conscious and took the girl. Then he made her sit. When the girl was seated, the Sun spoke to him again, saying, "Please stop fainting and listen to my words! When this daughter of yours gets married, take a brown cow-calf and tether her to a peg very early in the morning.*

---

* By having saved the girl the Sun has established with Aluel and her family a relationship which entitles the Sun to share in Aluel's bridewealth. If his request were not honored, a curse would befall Aluel. This would be so whether the Sun wished Aluel harm or not.

I will pick up the cow-calf on my way to the West."

"Very well!" said the father.

The day the girl was taken away from the Sun's home, a young man called Ring, who was very holy, saw it all in a vision.* His father had urged him to marry, but he had refused. His father was a very rich man. The day Ring saw the girl brought back home, he said, "Father!"

"Yes, my son," answered the father.

"The girl I have been waiting for has now returned to her home! So let the cattle be released for my bridewealth and we shall leave."

"My son," said his father, "how did you know about the girl?"

"I know," replied Ring, "Just let us go. The girl was in the home of the Sun, and now the Sun has just returned her to her father."

"Are you sure, my son?"

"Yes, Father!"

So the cattle were released. And they left. They spent three days on the way. Then seven days in all.

The day the girl was brought home, the father took out a bull and sacrificed it in the cattle-byre, all by himself.† Then he pulled the sacrificed beast out of the cattle-byre.

People were surprised. They wondered and asked him, "Chol, what killed the bull?"

"He was strangled by the rope," he said, "so I decided to slaughter him as he was dying anyway."

He also slaughtered goats and rams in sacrifice. When asked, he said they had also strangled themselves. All the sacrifices were to bless his daughter and he did not want people to know. No one in the village knew of her return; even the stepmother did not know.

Ring was on his way for seven days. On the seventh day, he arrived with his cattle. Nobody in the village knew about him. When the visitors arrived, they sat down.

The younger Aluel was by now a mature girl. When the visitors proposed marriage, the father thought that they had in mind the daughter who was at home and known to the people. He sat in front of his cattle-

---

* Certain holy men are believed to have supernatural powers which enable them to see what people do not ordinarily see.

† When a person has been away from home for long, sacrifices are made to bless his return.

byre; that was his usual sitting place. He called his wife and said, "Let special grain be ground and call all the neighbors to come and help you. The visitors are numerous."

He killed a bull for hospitality. Blood was cooked and brought. Ring, the bridegroom, then spoke and said: "The people will neither eat nor drink until the bride comes out to serve! Only when she serves water herself will the gentlemen drink." Ring then went to his prospective father-in-law and sat in front of him at the doorway of the cattle-byre and said, "Father!"

"Yes!" answered Chol.

"My age-set would like the bride herself to serve them water before they drink."

"But who do they want?" asked the father. "Did my daughter not serve them before?"

"No," said the bridegroom, "not that daughter."

"But what other daughter do I have?" asked the father.

"Yes, you have another daughter," Ring insisted. "People came for that other daughter and not for this daughter."

"My only other daughter," he said, "was lost. That is why you see me in this mourning condition."

"Yes," said Ring, "I know about her being lost. I even know where she was when she was said to be lost. I also know that she has been brought back and has been here for seven days. What cannot be is easily seen—you will not succeed in hiding her. We shall not leave her inside. Please let her come out to serve water to the age-set, so that people may begin to talk."

"But I have no daughter inside the cattle-byre," the father persisted. "If you came for a daughter other than the one already outside, then you will have to return with your cattle. I have no other girl."

When the bridegroom insisted, the father said, "Even if I had a girl as you say I do, how can I let her out? If I should let her out when no one in the village knows that she has come back, would it not be death you wish for her?* I have not even satisfied my longing for her and you want her to die!"

"Nothing will kill her," said the bridegroom.

---

* She might be bewitched to death by envious people.

"She cannot come out and survive," said the father. "Can't you understand that even the members of this village do not know she is here?"

"Unless she comes out," argued the bridegroom, "nothing will go well. How can you expect the age-set to stay without even drinking water?"

"Let the age-set drink water," said the father, "for if they mean to wait for this girl to come out, it will not happen."

They argued about it. The old man began to cry. The bridegroom persisted. The father continued to cry: "Is this what God willed for my daughter? The day she returns, she meets with death! Even the pleasure of having her back, I have not had time to enjoy fully. And now she is to die."

"Nothing will kill her," said the bridegroom. "Let her come out."

The old man just continued to cry. But then he went into the cattle-byre and addressed his daughter, "My daughter!"

"Yes, Father!"

"When God made your mother bear you and made her die the same day, then made you go away until you grew up, not allowing me to raise you myself, it was fate willed by God Himself. So come out and face that fate."

The girl had a jar she had brought from the house of the Sun. It was a jar for water. It was big. Her father told her to fill it with water and to take it with her.

As she emerged from the cattle-byre, people gently pinched one another to draw attention to her. When her stepmother saw her, she understood. She threw herself down and started to cry.

The porridge was cooking in the pot. The coarse flour was already added to the water and it was bubbling as it thickened the boiling water. The stepmother went and took the pot off the fire, saying that she was not going to cook any longer as long as there was a bride other than her own daughter. She covered herself with ashes as she cried, throwing herself on the ground.

Aluel took the water to the age-set and the marriage continued to be celebrated. The people spent about two or three days in the house. When everything was completed, they announced that they wanted to take their bride with them. But the father refused, saying, "You cannot take her now. If you want her, you better go and then come back to fetch her. To take her away now would be too painful. I have not yet satisfied my longing for her; depriving me of her right now would kill me."

"This cannot be," said the bridegroom. "She cannot remain because our home is too far. It took us seven days to reach here. We left our home the same day she left the house of the Sun."

"I cannot allow her to go," insisted the father.

They argued and argued. The old man became troubled. When the people tried to persuade him, he said, "I will not give my daughter away now. I would rather break the marriage."

His friends, age-mates, and neighbors came and pleaded with him, saying, "Chol, how can you reason like that? Can't you see that it is God's will that your daughter should not live with you? If God were not against your living with her, nothing would have made her lose her way and go after the Sun at an age when it was important for her to be with you and to grow up under your care until her marriage. If God has refused your living with her, then you should surrender and give her to her husband."

Thus the elders pleaded with him. So he surrendered his daughter.

While his daughter was still on her way to her marriage home, he killed his wife, as he then understood that it was she who had led his child astray.

The girl spent seven days on the way with her husband and his group, Then they arrived home.

The day they arrived, Ring's father saw her and said, "Ring, my son, please do not touch this girl as yet."

"What do you mean, Father?" asked Ring. "Are you thinking of the sacrifices that must first be made to ancestral spirits?"

"No," said the father. "She is my wife."

"Father," said Ring, "how could you think of such a thing? Even forgetting the insult to me, is it possible for you to wish my wife to be yours?"

"My son, I am not insulting you, I am speaking the truth. If you should touch this girl, I shall take it as a personal challenge; you would be looking for trouble!"

Ring slept and did not touch his wife. The girl also slept. The next day, his father spoke to him in the same way.

Then Ring said to his father, "Father, now that you speak that way, how do you want us to compete for the girl? Shall we do it with words or shall we do it by force?"

"We should fight," said the father, "and the one who will kill the other will take the girl for his wife! That she should go with you while I am alive, I will never accept. Ring, my son, do you really think that a beautiful girl like this should go with you while I am still alive?"

Ring, confounded by his father's words, remarked, "So, Father, you really mean what you have been saying?"

"Yes," replied the father, "I mean it! So if she is as dear to your heart as she is to me, then Ring, my son, I will kill my bull tomorrow morning and make a shield out of his skin. It will be for you to decide what you will do—whether to kill your mother to make a shield out of her skin or to go in search of a cow to kill for a shield."*

"If it is so important that you have my wife," said Ring, "then I will not kill my mother. Is it not better that I surrender the woman? How could your heart think of her and still be the father who begot me! It was you who arranged her marriage to me! If you now think that she is for you, and not for your son, then there is nothing I can do. You may have her."

Ring's mother overheard the conversation. She called her son and said, "Ring, my son, have you always been such a coward?"

"What do you mean?" asked Ring.

"How could you say that you are willing to leave your wife if it requires killing your mother? If you cannot face such a challenge from your father, the man who begot you, of what use can you be? If you cannot face the challenge of your father, be sure you will never be able to face the challenge of your age-mates."

"No, Mother," said Ring, "I cannot kill you! It is better that I leave the girl."

"That cannot be," said the mother. "You must kill me."

Ring's father went ahead and killed his bull and made his shield.

Ring talked of the matter with his mother for quite a while. Then he surrendered and agreed to fight his father.

The next morning, he woke up. His mother also came out of her hut very early. She said to him, "Ring!"

"Yes, Mother."

"When you have slaughtered me, skin me. Make half of my skin your

* Cattle are generally controlled by the head of the family. The son therefore has no independent wealth.

shield and leave the other half. Nobody knows what God will do. You may win your wife. And if you do, use the other half of my skin for sleeping with her."

Ring cried as he heard her speak.

His mother said, "Ring, my son, do not cry. Stop crying and kill me!"

Ring eventually took a spear and killed his mother. He slaughtered her. Then he skinned her. Half the skin, he kept. The other half he made into a shield. When his shield was finished, his father came and asked, "Ring, aren't you ready with your shield?"

"Yes," he said.

"And did you not kill your mother?"

"Yes, I did."

"In that case," continued his father, "let us meet tomorrow morning for our fight."

"Very well," said Ring.

The next day, his father woke up very early. He went and woke Ring. Ring got up and came to the place where they were to fight.

Ring had twin brothers born after him. Their names were Ngor and Chan. The morning of the fight, they also got up. Ngor stood behind his father and Chan stood behind his brother.

Ring and his father started to throw spears at one another. As his father would throw his spear, Ngor would say, "Father, please miss Ring!"

And when Ring would throw his spear, Chan would say, "Ring, please miss Father!"

They went on that way for quite a long time. They spent the whole morning fighting and neither hit the other.

When the sun became too hot, they stopped. In the late afternoon when the sun was cool, they resumed fighting, and the twins continued to ask them to miss one another. At nightfall, they stopped, and neither had hit the other.

The following morning, they began again and spent the day in the same way, fighting and missing according to the directions of the twins.

On the third day, Chan lost patience and got provoked. He said, "Ring, hit our father!"

Ring speared his father. It was a fatal hit. He killed him. As the father lay dying, he said, "Now that you have killed me, it is fitting that you go with the girl when I am dead. That she should be your wife when I was alive was impossible for me to accept." Ring went ahead and gave him a death blow. Then he buried him.

From the time that Ring killed his mother, his bride constantly cried. She took off all her ornaments to mourn her mother-in-law.

In the years to follow, she bore Ring many children. She had an equal number of boys and girls. Her children became so many that they were almost enough to hold a dance by themselves.

# Deng and His
# Vicious Stepmother

An old man called Chol had two wives. One was a daughter of a human being and the other was a daughter of a lion. The two wives conceived at the same time. They were pregnant. Then they delivered. The first to deliver was the lioness. The human wife delivered soon after. As soon as the human wife delivered, she became ill and died. Only the lioness remained.

The two children they had were both boys. One was called Deng and the other was also called Deng. The lioness took care of them both. She suckled them and raised them together. They became like twins. She raised them very carefully through all the stages: First they crawled, then they stopped being suckled, and then they walked.

The lioness had no more children. She stopped with that one child. Their father was still alive.

The boys grew and grew, until they could look after their sheep and goats. Then they grew older and could look after the calves. They continued to grow. Their father was still alive.

Then their father died suddenly. They remained with the lioness alone. All three of them lived together very happily. The lioness never even felt like a lioness. She was like a loving human being. She was an ideal mother to both of them.

They continued to grow until they became young men. Then they were initiated and became adults.

Whenever they went in search of girls, they went together. Neither of them would remain at home. That is how close they were. They were always together. Then they found two girl friends. One was called Achol and the other was also called Achol. The villages of the girls were near each other. The two men would go together whenever they wanted to visit their girl friends.

Deng of the human mother was betrothed to his girl friend. But she was still very young, she had not fully matured; she was still a child.

One day he said to Deng of the lioness, "Brother Deng, I would like to go and visit Achol."

"Very well," said Deng, "we will go!"

"No," said the other Deng, "I don't think we should continue to go together. No one remains to look after our cattle. They will be in the cattle-byre all alone. You must stay. Tomorrow I will look after the cattle while you visit your girl friend."

"Brother Deng," said Deng of the lioness, "I think you should not go alone. I must come with you."

Deng of the lioness had observed his mother lately and had noticed a change in her. It was as though she was developing an appetite for the human Deng.

"Brother Deng," he continued, "I am afraid for your safety. I have been watching my mother and I fear that if you go alone and I am in the cattle-byre, she might leave her sleeping-hut and follow you. I fear that she might harm you. So please let me come with you!"

"Don't be silly," said the human Deng. "How can she harm me after having raised me all this time as though she were my full mother?"

Deng, the son of the lioness, argued, and Deng of the human mother insisted. So his brother let him go alone.

He left. He walked. The lioness later went out of her hut while her son was in the cattle-byre. She caught up with the human Deng and began to walk by his side while hiding herself in the bush alongside the road.

Then she suddenly appeared, crossing the road in front of him. As soon as Deng recognized her, he put down his spears and sat on the ground.

Deng said to her, "Mother, if you want to eat me, then come do it. I will not defend myself. How could I do that? By killing you? Even if your heart has turned into that of a beast, and I now see you have become a beast, I will not hurt you. It is better you kill me and eat me without my resistance."

She teasingly put her teeth on him and said, "Deng, my son, how could I possibly eat you!"

She jumped into the bush and began walking secretly by his side. Then she suddenly jumped onto the road again. Once more, Deng laid down his spears and sat down. "Come, eat me!"

She again denied wanting to harm him and jumped into the bush.

They continued this way for quite a while. Eventually, she returned really wild. She jumped and plucked a gland from Deng's groin. He fell and remained on the ground. She jumped into the bush and disappeared with the gland. She returned to the village, taking it with her.

By this time, the village of Deng's girl friend, Achol, was quite near. The encounter with his stepmother had delayed him so much that it was now about midnight and too late for a normal visit to a girl friend.

Deng crawled towards Achol's village until he reached the doorway of the hut in which she slept. He then spoke. "People inside the hut, would you please tell me if Achol is there?"

Achol was the first to hear him. She said with excitement, "Listen, my people, I hear a voice like that of Deng outside the hut! Where could he have come from at this time of the night? This is not the time for a boy friend to visit. I don't think Deng is well. Something terrible must have happened. Even his voice sounds strange."

As she spoke, she was undoing the door. And although she was a little girl, she stepped out alone. She saw Deng with blood streaming from a wide-open wound where the gland had been. She went back into the hut crying, and took a fine piece of cotton. She soaked it in water and squeezed it into the wound. Then she boiled some water and gave Deng a hot bath.

Before daybreak, Deng said, "I must go!"

"How can you walk?" Achol asked.

"I can walk," he replied. "Do you think I would shame us by staying in your house to be found here in the morning? Of course not. Even if I were dying, I would have to leave before dawn."

"Please Deng, stay," she pleaded with him. "You cannot leave with this wound. I would understand what you are saying if you were well. What has honor to do with a person hurt like you?"

"I cannot agree with you. I must go."

He took a walking stick and limped away.

In the meantime, Deng of the lioness was extremely disturbed that his brother did not return all night. Very early in the morning, he took his spears and went after him. Before leaving, he talked to his mother and said, "If I find Deng with the slightest harm, you will be the one I will hold responsible."

His mother pretended to be shocked. "Deng, my son, how could you think such terrible thoughts? Is Deng a new person to me? What about the long time I spent raising him? If I wanted to harm him, would I have waited all this time? Can I now sacrifice so simply what I did with such great hardship? Can I destroy a child I bred with the milk of my breasts? How can I eat him?"

"I don't care what you say," said her son. "Deng has been too long away and it cannot be for nothing; something terrible must have happened."

"Well, go, and if you find that I have done him any harm, then come back to argue with me."

"Let me tell you, Mother," he said with emphasis, "I want you to know that if I find that you have done him the slightest harm, you will be in serious trouble with me."

"Go!"

Deng left. As he walked on the road, Deng of the human mother recognized him from a distance and thought to himself. "If Deng sees me suffering this way, he may do himself harm. I should hide."

So he went into the bush nearby and hid. Deng came and passed. Deng of the human mother saw him disappear and went back onto the road and limped on. He walked until he arrived home. He went into the cattle-byre and lay down on a mat, covering himself with another mat.

As it was still very early, his stepmother had returned to her hut to continue her sleep.

When Deng arrived at the village of Achol's family, Achol told him all about Deng.

"I knew it," he said, "I have been saying that something must have gone wrong because Deng would not stay at Achol's place all night into the next morning."

Then he ran back. He found Deng lying down, covered with the mat. When he asked him, Deng did not tell him anything—he simply said, "I am all right; it is just a small injury." But when he uncovered him and saw the wound, he went to his mother and said, "No one else but you did this. Wherever you have taken the gland, I want you to bring it and put it back where it was. Make it look as perfect as though nothing had happened. Otherwise, you are dead."

"My son," she said, "I did not do it."

"Don't talk. Put it back or I will kill you," he said as he raised his arm to pierce her with his spear.

"Stop," she cried, "don't kill me. I did not do it, but I will see what I can do to help him. Only don't think I did it; I am just helping him."

So she went and worked on Deng. She took out the cotton and put back the gland. She did it so well that it was as though nothing had happened.

They stayed together for a short while. Then Deng of the lioness went and said to his brother, "Deng!"

"Yes," he said.

"Let us face the truth that we are orphans. Your mother died when you were a newborn baby. Our father has also died. And my mother has turned into a beast. We might as well forget her. I want to kill her. I cannot allow her to live with us."

"No," said Deng, "you must not kill her."

"But if I don't kill her," continued Deng, "she might kill you. Then I will be without a brother. That I will not accept."

They argued and argued until Deng of the human mother gave in.

One evening, as the woman went into the hut, her son went and put dry grass all around the hut. Then he set the hut on fire. He took a black ram and threw it into the fire as a sacrifice to remove the curse of murder. His mother burned to death.

The brothers stayed for about two months. When the lioness' brother, who was a lion named Yor, heard the news of his sister's death, he came. He walked and walked, until he reached a small pool near the village of the two brothers. Yor did not really know where the village was. Nor did he know his sister's son. As he arrived at the pool, Deng, the son of his sister, was bathing in the pool. He said, "Young man, may I ask you a question?"

"Yes," Deng said.

"Where is the village of Deng, the son of the lioness?" asked the lion.

"There it is!" Deng answered.

"That one?" asked the lion.

"Yes," said Deng.

As soon as the lion stooped to pick up his spears, which he had laid down, Deng threw his fishing spear, hitting him fatally. As his uncle lay dying, Deng said to him, "My name is Deng. I am the son of your sister. You came to avenge your sister's death. You now see the cost. I have killed you."

"I see," said the dying lion. "Please kill me quickly. My son Miyar will avenge my death!"

Deng went ahead and killed him. Then he set the body on fire and threw a black ram into the fire as a sacrifice to remove the curse of murder.

The brothers Deng married their girl friends and went to live together in the same village. About a month later, Deng of the lioness called his brother and said, "Son of my father, lions have tricky ways. They may leave us in peace until we forget that we have a feud with them. My cousin Miyar, the son of the uncle I killed, is likely to surprise us and kill us. I think we should attack him first."

"Very well," agreed Deng.

They told their wives that they were leaving.

"Where are you going?" asked the women.

"We are going to the land of the lions," they answered.

"How can the two of you alone attack the land of the lions? Is it death you want? You are sure to die!"

"God will see to that," they said. "If we live, we live; if we die, we die."

Their women cried and tried to stop them, but all in vain. Their husbands would not be persuaded.

They took off their rings and said to the girls, "Keep these rings and observe them. If they rust, then we are dead. If they don't, then we are still alive. We shall now sing a song which we shall sing for you when we return. You will hear us sing it from a distance. Even if we arrive in the middle of the night, we shall wake you up with this song."

"Very well," said the women.

They proceeded to sing the song in a duet. Deng of the human mother began:

> "Land of the wilds, land of the wilds,
> A beast of a stepmother played jealousy on me.

Wife of my father, why did you do that to me
When I had no jealousy in my heart?
What misfortune befalls the child of a stepmother!"
His brother Deng took over:
"In a wild land I have never treaded,
I killed a big bull, my mother's brother,
And the great fighter steamed with burning fat,
Like the hut of my mother."
Their wives said, "Please sing it again so that we can recognize it on your
return." So Deng of the human being began again:
"Land of the wilds, land of the wilds,
A beast of a stepmother played jealousy on me.
Wife of my father, why did you do that to me
When I had no jealousy in my heart?
What misfortune befalls the child of a stepmother!"
His brother continued:
"In a wild land I have never treaded,
I killed a big bull, my mother's brother,
And the great fighter steamed with burning fat,
Like the hut of my mother."
Their wives then said, "Good, we now know it."
They left. They walked, and they walked, and they walked. They
would come to a lion-camp and Deng of the lioness would say, "Deng,
Brother, sing the song. There is no way for us to know the cattle-camp of
my mother's relatives. But if we sing and my uncle's son hears us, he will
know us and will come." Deng agreed and sang:
"Land of the wilds, land of the wilds,
A beast of a stepmother played jealousy on me.
Wife of my father, why did you do that to me
When I had no jealousy in my heart?
What misfortune befalls the child of a stepmother!"
His brother then sang:
"In a wild land I have never treaded,
I killed a big bull, my mother's brother,
And the great fighter steamed with burning fat,
Like the hut of my mother."

They walked and sang this way until they arrived at the camp of Miyar. The camp was well known in the area because Miyar was the chief. So it was pointed out to them. Then they sang near the camp:

"Land of the wilds, land of the wilds,
A beast of a stepmother played jealousy on me.
Wife of my father, why did you do that to me
When I had no jealousy in my heart?
What misfortune befalls the child of a stepmother!"

"In a land I have never treaded,
I killed a big bull, my mother's brother,
And the great fighter steamed with burning fat,
Like the hut of my mother."

Miyar asked the people to be silent. "Let me hear that song. Is that Deng singing? Has he really come? Who else could sing such a song?"

All the people became silent. The song was heard again and again. When Miyar was sure that it was Deng, he came out to meet him and said, "Is it you, Deng?"

"Yes," answered Deng.

Deng and his brother carried two axes, one small and one big, and a club. That is all they carried; they had no spears with them.

"Deng," said the lion. "What do you think we should do?"

"I think we should fight," replied Deng.

"Do you want me to go and turn wild?" asked Miyar.

"Go and turn wild!" said Deng.

"Perhaps I don't need to turn wild," his cousin said scornfully. "I will wrestle with you as though I were a human being. The person who throws the other down may kill him."

"If you prefer it that way," said Deng, "then let us wrestle."

They began to wrestle while Deng's human brother watched. They wrestled; they wrestled, and wrestled. Then Deng threw his cousin down. As soon as Miyar was down, the human Deng handed his wrestling brother one of the small axes. His brother hit the lion on the head. He split his head and killed him.

At that time, all the people who were in the cattle-camp ran away in panic. People shouted to their relatives and friends, "Please, wait for me."

But they would not. Some answered, "How can I wait for you when disaster has killed our Chief?" They all dispersed and disappeared, leaving only the cattle. There were horned cattle and hornless cattle. The hornless cattle turned into lions and lionesses and ran away with their owners.* Even the gourds containing the milk and the butter of the hornless cows ran into the forest. Only the cattle with horns remained.

A little boy and a little girl whom the lions had captured from human beings remained in the camp. The children were reduced to skin and bones by the lion's torture. Almost every day they would be bled and the lions would sip their blood.

The brothers Deng took them and all the remaining cattle and left for home. They walked, and they walked. They were delayed by the slow pace of the children, who were too big to be carried but too small to walk fast. The cattle, too, had to be driven slowly to graze on the way. So they walked and walked and walked.

They arrived at their village in the night. As they approached the village, Deng of the lioness asked his brother to sing. So he did:
"Land of the wilds, land of the wilds,
A beast of a stepmother played jealousy on me.
Wife of my father, why did you do that to me
When I had no jealousy in my heart?
What misfortune befalls the child of a stepmother!"
The other Deng sang his part:
"In a land I have never treaded,
I killed a big bull, my mother's brother,
And the great fighter steamed with burning fat,
Like the hut of my mother."
They listened and heard no response from the village. Deng of the lioness said, "I think they have not heard us. Why don't we sing it once more?" They sang it two more times.

During all this time, their wives were suffering from fear that they might have died. When days passed after they had expected them back, they despaired and started mourning.

* The Dinka believe that hornless cattle are generally more aggressive than cattle with horns. In folktales, hornless cattle usually follow their lion-owners and turn into lions, while cattle with horns remain normal.

As their husbands sang, one Achol heard their voices as though they were in a dream. To make sure she was not dreaming, she got up, listened some more, and then woke up the other Achol, and said, "Achol, wake up! Listen! There are our men singing!"

Achol said sleepily, "What wishful thinking! Do you really expect them to return again?"

"By God, may I die," she swore, "I hear men singing! Listen!"

They listened together. When they were sure it was their husbands' voices, they came out crying with joy and running to meet them. They seated them and gave them milk to drink. Each of the women wanted to cook. They argued about which of them should cook. Their husbands told them to stop. "Let one of you cook and the other will cook tomorrow." So one cooked. They also boiled some water to give the small children a hot bath.

And so they lived. The two brothers added their captured herd to their wealth and became very rich. They searched throughout the country for the parents of the children until they found the family of the boy. But they never found the relatives of the girl. So they adopted her as their sister and raised her until she was married. They received much bridewealth for her marriage and then gave her to her husband.

That is it; it is finished.

# Agany and His Search for a Wife

THIS IS AN ANCIENT EVENT.

A woman gave birth to many children. They were all girls. Not a single boy was among them. She reached the age when she could have no more children, without a boy.

The old man, her husband, would say, "What misfortune God has brought me. How can a man have so many children, all girls without a single son." He often complained that way.

One day he returned from the cattle-camp to visit his wife at home. Then she conceived despite her age. The baby grew very fast in her stomach.

He wondered, "I am confused by this woman. In the first place, how did she become pregnant at her age? And how can the baby grow so fast when she has just conceived? I cannot understand."

The baby continued to grow very rapidly. And within a short time, his wife gave birth. This time it was a boy.

The boy's skin was decorated in many colors. There was black skin, white skin, red skin—all these colors were on him. The father was puzzled.

He took out a bull and killed it in sacrifice. He also took out a ram and killed it. He then took out a second ram and killed it.

Then he sat and said, "I will just wait and see why God is doing this. Why He has at last given me a son without making him a normal human being, why He has colored his skin in this peculiar way, I cannot understand."

The baby was named Agany. He grew up very fast. He grew with every night that came. People were completely bewildered. Whenever his blanket was removed from him, people would run away in fear. No one dared to look at him closely.

His father was very rich. Each of his many daughters was married with many cattle and he kept all the cattle. So great was his wealth that he gave herds to relatives to help him take care of them. His brother-in-law kept a large stock. Each of his daughters also kept a large stock. And he himself remained with a large herd.

He kept his son at home. He would not take him out for the public to see.

In the meantime, Agany continued to grow very fast. That same year he grew so fast that he caught up with an age-set that was to be initiated. So he was initiated with that age-set.

The initiated group stayed in his house, and his family prepared food for the entire age-set. Women from the families of the other men stopped cooking altogether because their initiated relatives were served so much food in Agany's house.

Then they were released from initiation and went to the cattle-camp. Agany turned out to be an extremely handsome man who was popular with his age-mates as well as with the entire cattle-camp. He was especially popular with girls. Wherever he was, the girls of the camp all rushed over to have a glimpse of him. When there was a dance, he became the center of attraction. Even when he sat doing nothing, he drew everybody's attention.

All this bewildered Agany. He did not know what he should do about it.

When the cattle were released from the camp and he was seen displaying himself in the *goor*\* dance, no girl would leave the camp. Whenever a girl was sent away from the camp on an errand, she would say, "How can I leave the cattle-camp when Agany is dancing. That cannot be!"

Since his display would stop the activities of the cattle-camp, his father would ask him to stop. Then he would stop and sit.

When he was asked to get married, he refused, saying, "How can I know which girl to marry when they all behave alike towards me. Besides I understand that there is a plot by girls to kill whichever one I choose to

---

\* A dance form in which people act as though in actual battle, running in single file behind a leader, jumping up and down, twisting themselves as though dodging or throwing spears. It is often used as a prelude to ordinary dance. But it is also performed on other occasions for joy.

marry. How can I choose a girl and endanger her life? I cannot. It is better that I remain unmarried."

Each year came and the question of his marriage was raised, but he maintained his position and remained unmarried.

One year, he left his father in the cattle-camp and went to his mother at home. He told her that he had at last decided to marry, but had not yet made up his mind about the girl. He said he was returning to the cattle-camp for a few days and would come back to tell her of his success or failure in finding a girl.

He left her but did not return to the cattle-camp. Instead, he spent these days in the forest, hunting monitor lizards and skinning them. When he had collected a large number of skins, he made them into a suit exactly his shape, covering every part of him so that it looked like his own skin. He even made room for his fingers, toes, eyes, every part of him. Then he tried it on and worked on it some more until it fitted him perfectly.

Then he returned to the cattle-camp. He went to his father and said, "It is now in my heart to marry. I shall leave to look for a wife. For my journey, I would like two milk-gourds to be cleaned and filled with milk."

Two gourds were cleaned and left in the sun to dry. Then they were filled with milk. He took his skin, wrapped it carefully, and tied it to a stick. He took his milk-gourds and also tied them to the stick. Then he placed the stick on his shoulder.

He walked and walked until it was dark. Then he put down his load, sat down, and drank some milk. Afterwards, he went to the top of a tree to spend the night safe from wild animals. He slept until dawn.

Very early the next morning, he put his load on his shoulder and left. He walked and walked and walked, until it was dark again. He stopped for the night and slept.

The next morning he again left very early. He walked and slept for a third night on the way.

On the fourth day, he arrived at a large cattle-camp at about the time when the cattle were returning from their day's grazing. He saw many girls on the edge of the cattle-camp. Some girls were pounding their grain. Others were cleaning their utensils. And still others were fetching water from the river. He hid and put on his skin. He speared a frog, went back to the camp with the frog, and approached one girl, begging her, "Girl, would you please cook this frog for me?"*

The girl, disgusted with his skin and the frog, shouted back, "Get away, you monitor-lizard-looking creature! Have you ever seen your kind honored by a girl? How can anyone cook for a person like you?"

He left that girl and went to another one: "Girl, would you please give me some water?"

She laughed at him and said, "Look at this monitor-lizard-looking creature! How can you expect me to give you water?"

He went around the camp begging help from the girls and being rebuked until he had approached nearly all the girls in the camp.

Then he came to the family of an elderly couple. He found an old woman, called after her eldest daughter, Ayom's Mother. Her daughters, Ayom and her three sisters, were pounding grain. Nearby was another little girl, also their sister, called Aluat. Aluat was an extremely beautiful girl but she was still a child.

As soon as the older girls saw the man, they chased him away: "Be off and do not stop or look back!"

Aluat, who had taken the gourds to her family's compound in the cattle-camp, saw her sisters speaking rudely to the man. As she saw the man leave, she ran towards her sisters and said, "Ayom, where did that man you were rebuking come from?"

Her eldest sister, Ayom, immediately retorted, "You with your search for trouble! Have you seen what he looks like?"

"He looks like a human being to me," said Aluat.

"He wants someone to cook a frog for him!" explained one of her sisters.

"In that case," responded Aluat, "let me go and take it. I shall cook it for him."

She ran after the man, calling to him as she ran. When he heard her, he stopped and looked back. When she reached him, he asked, "What do you want from me?"

"I came," she explained, "because I saw you talk with my sisters and leave in a disappointed way. So I thought I would ask you to tell me what

---

* For the Dinka, who do not eat frogs, to think of eating a frog is despicable.

you wanted and whether I could help you. At least, see whether I will answer like my sisters."

"Is that why you came after me?" asked Agany.

"Yes!" she said.

"Well, I was looking for someone to cook this frog for me!"

"Then give it to me," she said.

He gave her the frog. She took the frog to her compound and then returned to him. She led him to a different part of the camp where her best friend, a little girl of her own age called Ayan, was. She called on her and said, "Ayan, this man is a traveller. I would like him to sit here in your place because ours is too exposed and people tend to fear him. I would rather he stayed in a less open place."

Ayan accepted and seated Agany.

Aluat then returned to her family and told her father about the man. "Father," she said, "a man came here before. When he asked your daughters for help, they sent him away. So I went and took him to the other side of the camp. But I would like to take some milk to him."

Her father allowed her to do so. But when her older sister heard what she said, she became enraged: "Do you have to entertain any creature that crosses your way? I don't think you should take up with this man!"

But her father insisted that cows be milked and the milk given Aluat to take to the man. The cows were milked and she took the milk to Agany.

By that time, her girl friend, Ayan, had taken leave. So they were left alone. Then Agany spoke to Aluat and said, "Aluat, what you see is not my real body. Although the skin you see on me is ugly and poor, I have a different skin under that, the skin God created for me. So, take back your milk, my interest in you forbids my drinking it.* After returning the milk, please come back. I will tell you the rest."

Aluat said that she would have to get permission from her father before coming back. "I am a little girl," she said, "and my father will be disturbed if I stay out late without his permission."

Agany agreed and Aluat went to her side of the camp. She went and

---

* Among the Dinka a man does not eat or drink in the house of his girl friend. And even after marriage a certain ceremony must be performed before a bridegroom may eat among his wife's family.

sat near her father and said, "Father, the man wants me to return to him and I would like to go. May I?"

"Yes, you may," said her father.

So she went. When she was with him, he said to her, "Make a fire so that you may see my real body. But when you have seen me, you must not tell anybody. You must keep the truth to yourself. The rest of the people will see me when I return in the future. Now let me tell you that I have come in search of a wife. Even if she is very young, if she has the character I have been searching for, she is the one I want. If an older woman had behaved the way you did, I would have shown myself to her and asked for her in marriage."

The girl kindled the fire and saw his real body. She was amazed and silent for some time, and then she left.

The following day Agany picked up his gourds and left early in the morning. He spent the same number of days he had spent on his way from home. Then he arrived at his cattle-camp.

He went and spoke to his father, saying, "Father, I have found a girl. She is still a very small girl, but she is good-natured and beautiful. I was not really after beauty; I was after a girl with a good heart, a girl who would not despise a human being no matter how ugly he might be. I have found her. So I will now marry."

"Son," said his father, "I was always for you marrying; you were the one refusing. So if you have now found the girl of your choice, I am exceedingly glad."

Agany's age-mates in the cattle-camp were called and three bulls were brought out and slaughtered for a feast. One hundred cows and ten bulls were released to be taken to Aluat's family as bridewealth. Agany and his age-mates drove the cattle. Together with the cattle were oxen to be slaughtered on the way for meat. There were also cows to provide milk on the way. As the men drove the cattle slowly, they spent many days on the way. They would go some distance and stop. They would tether the cattle and make them rest. When they reached the territory of Aluat's family, they found that the cattle had been moved from the camp to the villages. As they travelled, people wondered, "Where is this large cattle-camp going?"

People would answer, "It is not a cattle-camp; these are bridewealth cattle!"

"Whose daughter is being married?"

"The girl is to be found where the cattle are being taken. No one but the husband-to-be has as yet seen the girl."

Onlookers would say, "What a lucky man to receive so many beautiful cattle for his daughter. She must be a very beautiful girl. What else would a father wish for?"

People kept asking these questions all along the way until the visitors arrived at the bride's home. The visitors asked, "Is the senior gentleman by the name of Ayom's Father at home?"*

A village was pointed out to them: "That is the village of Ayom's Father. It will not take you much longer to reach there."

Agany began to run in the *goor* dance, accompanied by specially decorated oxen. Some men danced and some sang over the oxen as they entered the homestead. The elderly gentleman came out to meet them. The visitors spoke to him, saying, "Father of Ayom, we are your guests."

"What guests are you?" he asked.

"We are marriage guests," they answered.

"And the girl?"

"We do not know the girl," they said. "Only the bridegroom does. But we shall tell you tomorrow after a good night's sleep."

"Very well," he said. Once he knew the bridegroom, he knew he had come for his little girl, Aluat. The word went around that the monitor-lizard man had returned for Aluat.

Ayom's Father welcomed the guests and seated them. He brought out four bulls from his cattle-byre and slaughtered them in hospitality. Plenty of food was prepared. And the people slept.

The bridegroom was in his monitor lizard's suit. Some people wondered, "How can a monitor-lizard man come and ask for our Aluat? Such an ugly man! It will never be! Whatever his wealth, we must refuse."

The girl, Aluat, knew what he really looked like because she had seen him, but she remained silent.

The morning came. People gossiped and waited, but nothing happened. Many became very impatient. Some longed for the sun to set because the evening was the time when gentlemen were to meet with young ladies and

---

* As a matter of courtesy, the Dinka often refer to men and women by the names of their first-borns, male or female.

discuss the question of courtship. Girls from the neighboring areas were invited. They all came.

People still argued that Aluat should not be given to the monitor-lizard man, whatever amount and quality of cattle he had. "Such an ugly man! Such a coarse skin! This cannot be! He cannot take our Aluat. What are cattle compared to our fine Aluat? We do not care about wealth; it is Aluat who matters to us. We will never agree to this proposal!"

Agany's age-mates became impatient with this insulting talk. "Now, Agany," they said, "we have had enough of this abuse. Reveal yourself! You have brought scorn and disrespect on us. Show yourself!"

"Very well," said Agany, "I will reveal myself."

It was night. Agany said, "Make three huge heaps of straw and set them on fire so that you may have sufficient light to see my body!"

The heaps were made and lit. Agany stood in the middle of the three huge fires. He then stripped the skin of the monitor lizard off his body and said, "Now see me, whether I am ugly or handsome."

The girls began disputing, each one crying, "He is for me." "He is mine." "I want him." Even Aluat's eldest sister made her claim. "This man is not for the little girl, Aluat. He is for me, the eldest!"

All the evening activities turned into a fight over Agany.

The next morning, he woke up and danced the *goor* in front of Aluat's mother's hut. The age-set ate the feast. The festivities went on for days. Then the guests were ready to leave.

Agany spoke to Aluat's father and said, "Father, I came all the way here to avoid the sort of competition among girls that happened last night. That is what drove me away from my own territory. I come from a very distant village. Your daughter Aluat, whom I am marrying, is a small child. That is why I cannot take her now. If she were old enough, she would not stay here. I would take her to my home. But her age has stopped me. I am leaving her, but I am making a special request for you to take very good care of her. For I am afraid that I might lose her."

"Don't worry," said the father, "I will look after her."

The age-set then left, and the father took special care of his daughter.

The following year, Agany said to his father, "Father, I must leave. My heart is heavy. I fear that something may have happened to Aluat. So I must go to see her. Whether she has grown up or is still small, I shall not leave her behind this time."

His father agreed. And he left for Aluat's home.

In the meantime, Aluat had trouble in the cattle-camp. Whatever a girl said, she was humiliated in comparison to Aluat: "Who do you think you are? Aluat, the girl married by Agany?" This became too much for most girls. The girls of the camp came to resent Aluat and her marriage. They got together and schemed to do away with Aluat. They announced that they were going to collect wild fruits. Girls throughout the cattle-camp got together and left. They walked and walked, until they were very far from the cattle-camp.

Then they said, "Aluat, we are very thirsty. That is the river over there where there is a cluster of big trees. You are the youngest and therefore the proper one to send. Please go and fetch us water!"

"With what shall I bring you water?" Aluat asked.

"Why don't you just go," they said. "Perhaps you will find some containers there. If not, we shall then go ourselves!"

"All right," she said and left.

They watched her go until she disappeared. Then the girls dispersed. They returned to the camp. Only her best friend, Ayan, remained.

Ayan followed Aluat, running and shouting after her. When she caught up with her, she said, "Aluat, why are you heading for the wilderness? Don't you understand what the girls have done to you? All this was a plan to lead you astray. We may never be able to trace our way back, but we must try."

As they began their journey back, the sun went down. They became confused and did not know what to do.

All the other girls reached the cattle-camp. When Aluat's father heard of his daughter's absence, he cried and cried: "This is exactly what I was warned against! Now the girls of our camp have proved Agany's suspicion to have been right!"

The two girls struggled to find the way back. One would go this direction and the other that direction and they would both meet going the same way. So confused did they become that they decided to spend the night on top of a tree.

As soon as they were on top of the tree, a lion came. He smelt them from under the tree but could not see anyone around. He wondered, "What is this human smell without a human being around?" Then he would look around and into the distance. He would look up to the top of the tree. But he saw no one. He waited and waited, deep into the night, and then gave up.

The girls spent the night in the tree. Early the next morning they descended from the tree and left. They eventually managed to find their way back to the cattle-camp, partly guided by the bellows of the cattle.

When they were seen, it was a very great event. After the story was told by Aluat and Ayan, each brother seized a whip and beat his sister for the wrong she had done. Aluat's father had become mad from grief and had been chained. He was then released.

In the meantime, Agany had left his home and was on the way. He arrived after the girls had returned. When he was told what had happened, in his unhappiness he said, "This is just why I left my own territory and came here to look for a wife. Now it has followed me into your territory! What a misfortune!"

He was told of what Ayan had done to save Aluat's life.

Then he spoke to Aluat's father and said, "Father, I must go. But I cannot leave Aluat behind again. As for Ayan, I would like you to speak to her father. She should be with Aluat, I will not leave her; I will keep her with Aluat. I will therefore be back, but I must now leave."

He left with Aluat and built a large home for her. Then he took out fifty cows, drove them to Ayan's father, married Ayan, and brought her home. He continued marrying into that cattle-camp, paying twenty, thirty, or forty cows for each girl until he had an enormous family. Then he said that Aluat and Ayan were not to pound grain, fetch water, or do any menial work; they were to bear him children to make up for his lack of brothers. His cattle were then divided between his wives. Some got only one cow; others got two; lucky ones had four cows. That way he distributed his wealth and maintained his wives. As he had wished, Aluat and Ayan had sons for their first-born children.

# Chol and His Baby-Bride

An elderly man called Deng had lived for a long time without marrying. He spent his life taking care of cattle. Then he decided to betrothe a small girl who had not yet reached the age of puberty. When the girl reached puberty, he completed the marriage and she was given to him. His bride remained for a long time without conceiving. She was held by *agorot*, the spirit of procreation.*

In a nearby village there was a young man called Chol who was his father's only child. Chol's father urged him to marry, but he refused, saying, "I do not want to marry."

"Why?" asked his father.

"I have not yet found the girl of my heart," Chol answered. "When I find her, I shall marry." This went on for many years.

His father's wealth was enormous. His father kept pleading with him, "Son, please marry. You will disappear childless and perish forever."

He would say, "No, Father, I do not want to marry." Eventually his father gave up and never asked him again.

Meanwhile, the wife of the elderly man still had not conceived. But when her husband made a sacrifice to her *agorot*, she conceived.

Since their villages were near, Chol knew about her childlessness and her eventual pregnancy. When she was about to deliver, Chol heard about

---

* Girls who are engaged before puberty are believed to be possessed by a spirit called *agorot*, which must be propitiated; otherwise the woman remains childless or her children will die.

69

it, and when the woman was in labor, he went into her hut and sat by her side among the women.

This was surprising to everyone. He was a young handsome man wearing a large ivory bangle on his arm.

People wondered, "How can such a gentleman come and sit with women in a hut in which a woman is giving birth. This is amazing!"

As he sat watching, he took off his ornaments, including the ivory bangle on his arm.

Again people wondered, "What has happened to Chol? Why is he stripping himself of beads and bangles as though in mourning?"

He continued to sit there as the woman was in labor. The woman delivered a baby girl. As soon as the baby was out and had its cord cut from its mother, Chol went closer to the woman and said, "Please give me the baby!"

Amazed by his conduct, people raised their voices in bewilderment, "Why? What are you doing? What has befallen you, Chol?"

"It is my wish; that is all," was his response to their pleading.

"How can the baby be given to you before the blood is washed off her body?"

"Yes," he insisted, "just give her to me."

People could not believe what they saw. "Has Chol gone mad or has he simply become an idiot?" they would ask. "No sane man could think of such a thing."

Chol sat and did not reply to their insults.

People were absolutely baffled and did not know what to do. Some people said, "Let her be given to him; let us see just what he is up to!"

He held the baby and placed her on his lap. Her mother was a step away from him and the baby.

Chol stayed, holding the baby, until he was told to give her to the mother to be breast fed. He handed the baby over to the mother. The baby was suckled. When she finished, Chol asked for her to be handed back to him. The baby was given back to him.

So surprised were the people by his behavior that it was thought difficult to deny him his wish.

For days and days, he stayed with the woman and the baby. Even at night, it was he who took care of the baby, and the mother looked on.

Chol refused to eat or drink in the baby's house.* His water and food were brought from outside the village.

The baby was given the name Atholong.

Word reached Chol's father that his son was behaving strangely. Chol's father decided to distribute the cattle he had kept for Chol's marriage, saying, "He is no longer of use to me. So it was this idiocy which kept my son from marriage! To look after newborn babies—what shame! There is nothing I can do. I will give my cattle away. If it is God's will that my lineage should perish, so be it."

He gave some of his cattle to his sister's children, some to the children of his maternal uncle, and some to the children of many other relatives.

Chol was left without cattle. But he did not care. He never even spoke of what his father was doing. He remained in the house, taking care of the baby. He stayed there until the baby could lie on its stomach. Then she could be seated while he sat near to support her. When the baby was sufficiently grown to sit alone, he said he wanted to take her to the cattle-camp.

The mother of the child came to look upon Chol as though he were the father. She said, "How can you look after the baby alone? Newly weaned babies are so difficult to take care of!"

"It doesn't matter," he said. "I will go with her and I will take good care of her."

The baby's father intervened and said, "All is well, let him take the child."

So Chol went with the baby to the cattle-camp.

The baby's family produced two cows for the baby's milk. Chol went to his mother's relatives and obtained a milk cow. This cow provided him with milk since he would not drink the milk of the other cows.

They lived together in the camp for a long time. The child became so fond of him that whenever he left her, even though for a short time, she cried. She would not eat or drink milk unless he was with her.

He would take her with him into the company of men. Sometimes he would just sit with her alone under a separate tree.

The child grew and grew in his company until she was quite a big girl, but she had not yet reached the age of puberty. Chol went home to the girl's father and said, "Father!"

* See the footnote on page 63, *Agany and His Search for a Wife.*

"Yes," said the man.

"When I was living here in your house, many terrible things were said against me. I was accused of madness and idiocy, but I never replied to the insults. As you know, my father has given away all my cattle. He thought of me as nobody. All this happened because I was after what my heart wanted. It is now a very long time since I was born. My age-mates at present have children. It was not that I had no cattle. It was I who was refusing. My refusal, combined with what I did in your house, led my father into thinking that I had become an imbecile. I am not an imbecile. There is not the slightest imbecility in me. It is just that my heart wanted it that way. So what I am here to tell you is that I would like to marry the little girl I was looking after."

"Son," answered the elder, "how can you think of that? Does not your raising her make you like her father?"

"But that is the very reason I raised her. The fact that I took her into my hands the minute her mother bore her and continued to look after her must have shown to you that I had intended to marry her!"

The elder said, "If that is your wish my son, there is nothing wrong with it. You may have her."

So he paid some cows for betrothal.*

The girl had already become betrothed to Chol's best friend. The two became bitter competitors, but both the girl's father and Chol knew that she would ultimately be Chol's wife. She was still below the age of puberty. But she had turned out to be extremely beautiful. She was the most beautiful girl in the cattle-camp.

A lioness-girl called Aluel heard of her famed beauty. She went to her cattle-camp. She would hide outside the camp waiting to attack the girl by stealth.

By this time, Chol had returned to his cattle-camp. He did not ask for his cattle to be returned to him. He only owned that one cow his mother's brother had given him. When that cow became dry, his mother's brother sent another milk cow for him. He never asked his father for anything.

But finally, he went to his father and said, "Father!"

"Yes," responded his father.

* As many relatives and friends assist in the payment of bridewealth, Chol's father's disposal of Chol's cattle did not necessarily leave Chol without cattle to pay for his marriage.

"You said I had become an idiot and gave away all my cattle. What shall we do now?"

"What do you mean?" asked his father. "Chol, my son, can you really deny being an idiot? Have you ever heard of a man holding a newly born baby? Would it not frighten anyone but an idiot to do so? Because you held the baby and refused to marry for so long, I became convinced that you were an idiot."

"What made me take off my ornaments and hold a newborn baby," said Chol, "was the same thing that kept me from marrying. I had told you that my reason for not marrying was that I had not found the girl of my heart. But when I heard that *that* woman was going to give birth, I went in the hope that it would be a girl, and God made her a girl. I took her and raised her. I raised her because my heart loved her from the start. Now I want her to be my wife! I want to marry her."

"So that was the reason," said his father.

"Yes!" said Chol.

"Well," said his father, "your cows are with other people, but they are not lost. It is for you to reclaim them. If I am wrong in thinking you an idiot, then you are entitled to your cattle."

"I am glad," said Chol.

In the meantime, the lioness-girl was still after Atholong. She continued to lie in hiding, hoping that the girl would come passing by. Nobody knew this.

One night Atholong went out to the edge of the cattle-camp. The lioness grabbed her and ran away with her. The lioness was so wild that she could fly. She took her into a thicket in the bush.

She was so attracted by the girl that whenever she wanted to eat her, she would look at her and change her mind and say, "O, what beauty; I will eat her tomorrow!" She would then go and hunt for animal flesh. She would return and give Atholong meat and whatever else she wanted. They lived together for quite a while. Each day came and she put off killing her.

The warrior age-set in the cattle-camp decided to go out searching for Atholong. They searched and searched until they found her.

Throughout all this period, Atholong would sing when the lioness was away:

"Father, Father!
Mother! Father!
Why did you delay the marriage?
Mother! Father!
Is this what you wanted?
And you said it was because of my *agorot*
Atholong has disappeared!''
The lioness would hear her in the forest and sing back:
"Your husband, Chol, is coming!
Chol, the Spearer of the Nile Perch, is coming!''
The girl would answer back:
"Chol is not coming!
O no! Chol is not coming!''
And that is the way they lived. Then the age-set arrived. As the people approached, the lioness emerged with immense ferocity. The age-set became frightened and returned to the camp.

The man who first betrothed Atholong sharpened his spears and went to meet the lioness. When he saw her, he too became afraid. He withdrew and returned to the camp.

In the meantime, Chol remained silent; he never said anything about what happened. But when he saw that everybody had gone and returned in fear, he gathered all their spears, including their fishing spears, and sharpened them. Then he left.

That was the day the lioness had made up her mind to eat the girl. She kept coming back to attack her, but each time she would put off Atholong's death, saying, "There is just one more thing to do. Let me pile up more grass so that the sand does not touch her beautiful skin! Perhaps I should find something even smoother to lay her on as I eat her!''

Atholong would sing, the lioness would reply, and Atholong would answer back.

Then the lioness went to cut down trees in order to make a platform on which to lay Atholong when she ate her, so that the girl would not be touched by dirt. Then the girl would sing, the lioness would respond, and the girl would answer back.

The lioness said to herself: "Why am I not eating her? Is it perhaps Chol who has done magic on me so that he will arrive before I eat the girl?

I will not allow this to happen! I will make sure I eat her before he arrives."

Meanwhile, Chol was on his way. He was very close to the place where Atholong was. He could even hear her faintly.

After making the platform, the lioness went and cut some more grass to put on top of the platform to make it even more comfortable. The girl sang, the lioness responded, and the girl sang back.

At the moment she finished her song, Chol appeared. The lioness had just finished piling more grass on the platform upon which she was to eat Atholong. She turned to find that Chol had just arrived.

At that point, Atholong spoke and said, "Chol, is it really you?"

"Yes," said Chol, "it is me!"

"What are you coming for? It is better that we do not both die. I am already a dead person. It is better that you remain alive even if I die. If you and I both die, it will not help anybody!"

Chol said, "My heart is sweetened, for I have found you still alive. Even if we both die, let us now die together!"

"No," she said, "that is not right."

The lioness then spoke to Chol and said, "Chol, have you arrived?"

"Yes, I have," said Chol.

"I knew you would come," she said. "I never forgot you. Wait for me. I will go and turn wild!"

"All right," said Chol. "Go and turn wild!"

"I will!" she said as she went away. She did not go far, nor did she turn completely wild. She just went nearby and returned.

Chol said, "You have not turned wild. You had better become really wild before I fight you!"

"Is that what you want?" she asked.

"Yes," he answered.

She left. Then she returned, a long, red, quivering tongue hanging from her mouth. But Chol said to her, "You are not really wild; go back and become really wild!"

Again, she left. She returned this time with a green, quivering tongue. But Chol said to her, "You are not really wild; go back and become really wild!"

Then she returned with a dark grey tongue, almost black, and was steaming hot. Chol took a small spear out of his collection and speared her.

He hit a fatal spot and forced her to the ground. As she lay dying, she said, "Chol!"

"Yes," answered Chol.

"Have you really killed me?"

"Yes, I have," replied Chol.

"Yes, I knew you would take my life. I knew you would kill me. This girl will go with you! She will be your wife. Nothing else will befall her. In the future, when you are husband and wife, she will bear you children—many children. Her children alone will be enough to hold a dance. Your first-born will be a girl. When she marries, take a small calf, raise it to be known as mine. If it is slaughtered for me, that too would be good. That will guarantee good health for you and your children and will make your wife produce many children."

"Very well," said Chol, "we shall do as you say."

He went ahead and gave her a death blow. Then he left with Atholong to return home.

Atholong's father and mother had despaired. When Chol brought her back, her father said, "If Chol has brought my daughter back, I will give her to him without payment. I will not have to be paid any cattle for her marriage."

But Chol refused and said, "This cannot be. It has been a very long time since I first held her and raised her to be a woman. I cannot take her without giving proper payment of cattle. That would be a shame on her and on me. My bringing her from death is small compared to everything else I have intended for her. I must marry her with cattle."

In the meantime, Chol's father reclaimed the cattle he had given away, brought them and gave them to Chol. So Chol paid the bridewealth and completed the marriage. He was then given his wife and the man who had first betrothed the girl was compensated.

Atholong went and gave birth to a daughter. After that, she had sons. She continued to bear children; so many that her children were enough to complete a dance all alone. She was very happy with her husband. When their first daughter was married, they took out a calf and dedicated it to the lioness.

That is my story.

# Diirawic and Her Incestuous Brother

THIS IS AN ANCIENT EVENT.

A girl called Diirawic was extremely beautiful. All the girls of the tribe listened to her words. Old women all listened to her words. Small children all listened to her words. Even old men all listened to her words. A man called Teeng wanted to marry her, but her brother, who was also called Teeng, refused. Many people each offered a hundred cows for her bride-wealth, but her brother refused. One day Teeng spoke to his mother and said, "I would like to marry my sister Diirawic."

His mother said, "I have never heard of such a thing. You should go and ask your father."

He went to his father and said, "Father, I would like to marry my sister."

His father said, "My son, I have never heard of such a thing. A man marrying his sister is something I cannot even speak about. You had better go and ask your mother's brother."

He went to his mother's brother and said, "Uncle, I would like to marry my sister."

His maternal uncle exclaimed, "My goodness! Has anybody ever married his sister? Is that why you have always opposed her marriage? Was it because you had it in your heart to marry her yourself? I have never heard of such a thing! But what did your mother say about this?"

"My mother told me to ask my father. I agreed and went to my father. My father said he had never heard such a thing and told me to come to you."

"If you want my opinion," said his uncle, "I think you should ask your father's sister."

78

He went around to all his relatives that way. Each one expressed surprise and suggested that he should ask another. Then he came to his mother's sister and said, "Aunt, I would like to marry my sister."

She said, "My child, if you prevented your sister from being married because you wanted her, what can I say! Marry her if that is your wish. She is your sister."

Diirawic did not know about this. One day she called all the girls and said, "Girls, let us go fishing." Her words were always listened to by everyone, and when she asked for anything, everyone obeyed. So all the girls went, including little children. They went and fished.

In the meantime, her brother Teeng took out his favorite ox, Mijok, and slaughtered it for a feast. He was very happy that he was allowed to marry his sister. All the people came to the feast.

Although Diirawic did not know her brother's plans, her little sister had overheard the conversation and knew what was happening. But she kept silent; she did not say anything.

A kite flew down and grabbed up the tail of Teeng's ox, Mijok. Then it flew to the river where Diirawic was fishing and dropped it in her lap. She looked at the tail and recognized it. "This looks like the tail of my brother's ox, Mijok," she said. "What has killed him? I left him tethered and alive!"

The girls tried to console her, saying, "Diirawic, tails are all the same. But if it is the tail of Mijok, then perhaps some important guests have arrived. It may be that they are people wanting to marry you. Teeng may have decided to honor them with his favorite ox. Nothing bad has happened."

Diirawic was still troubled. She stopped the fishing and suggested that they return to find out what had happened to her brother's ox.

They went back. As they arrived, the little sister of Diirawic came running to her and embraced her, saying, "My dear sister Diirawic, do you know what has happened?"

"I don't know," said Diirawic.

"Then I will tell you a secret," continued her sister, "but please don't mention it to any one, not even to our mother."

"Come on, Sister, tell me," said Diirawic.

"Teeng has been preventing you from being married because *he* wants to marry you," her sister said. "He has slaughtered his ox, Mijok, to celebrate his engagement to you. Mijok is dead."

Diirawic cried and said, "So that is why God made the kite fly with Mijok's tail and drop it in my lap. So be it. There is nothing I can do."

"Sister," said her little sister, "let me continue with what I have to tell you. When your brother bedevils you and forgets that you are his sister, what do you do? I found a knife for you. He will want you to sleep with him in the hut. Hide the knife near the bed. And at night when he is fast asleep, cut off his testicles. He will die. And he will not be able to do anything to you."

"Sister," said Diirawic, "you have given me good advice."

Diirawic kept the secret and did not tell the girls what had occurred. But she cried whenever she was alone.

She went and milked the cows. People drank the milk. But when Teeng was given milk, he refused. And when he was given food, he refused. His heart was on his sister. That is where his heart was.

At bedtime, he said, "I would like to sleep in that hut. Diirawic, Sister, let us share the hut."

Diirawic said, "Nothing is bad, my brother. We can share the hut."

They did. Their little sister also insisted on sleeping with them in the hut. So she slept on the other side of the hut. In the middle of the night, Teeng got up and moved the way men do! At that moment, a lizard spoke and said, "Come, Teeng, have you really become an imbecile? How can you behave like that towards your sister?"

He felt ashamed and lay down. He waited for a while and then got up again. And when he tried to do what men do, the grass on the thatching spoke and said, "What an imbecile! How can you forget that she is your sister?"

He felt ashamed and cooled down. This time, he waited much longer. Then his desire rose and he got up. The rafters spoke and said, "O, the man has really become an idiot! How can your heart be on your mother's daughter's body? Have you become a hopeless imbecile?"

He cooled down. This time he remained quiet for a very long time, but then his mind returned to it again.

This went on until very close to dawn. Then he reached that point when a man's heart fails him. The walls spoke and said, "You monkey of a human being, what are you doing?'' The utensils rebuked him. The rats in the hut laughed at him. Everything started shouting at him. "Teeng, imbecile, what are you doing to your sister?''

At that moment, he fell back ashamed and exhausted and fell into a deep sleep.

The little girl got up and woke her older sister, saying, "You fool, don't you see he is now sleeping? This is the time to cut off his testicles.''

Diirawic got up and cut them off. Teeng died.

Then the two girls got up and beat the drums in a way that told everybody that there was an exclusive dance for girls. No men could attend that dance. Nor could married women and children. So all the girls came out running from their huts and went to the dance.

Diirawic then spoke to them and said, "Sisters, I called you to say that I am going into the wilderness.'' She then went on to explain to them the whole story and ended, "I did not want to leave you in secret. So I wanted a chance to bid you farewell before leaving.''

All the girls decided they would not remain behind.

"If your brother did it to you,'' they argued, "what is the guarantee that our brothers will not do it to us? We must all leave together!''

So all the girls of the tribe decided to go. Only very small girls remained.

As they left, the little sister of Diirawic said, "I want to go with you.''

But they would not let her. "You are too young,'' they said, "you must stay.''

"In that case,'' she said, "I will cry out loud and tell everyone your plan!'' And she started to cry out.

"Hush, hush,'' said the girls. Then turning to Diirawic they said, "Let her come with us. She is a girl with a heart.* She has already taken our side. If we die, we die together with her!''

Diirawic accepted and they went. They walked; they walked and walked and walked, until they came to the borders between the human territory and the lion world. They carried their axes and their spears; they had everything they might need.

They divided the work among themselves. Some cut the timber for

---

* Among the Dinka, the functions of the heart and the mind are conceptually fused. This expression therefore means wise, prudent, discreet, considerate, and the like.

rafters and poles. Others cut the grass for thatching. And they built for themselves an enormous house—a house far larger even than a cattle-byre. The number of girls was tremendous. They built many beds for themselves inside the hut and made a very strong door to make sure of their safety.

Their only problem was that they had no food. But they found a large anthill, full of dried meat, grain, and all the other foodstuffs that they needed. They wondered where all this could have come from. But Diirawic explained to them. "Sisters, we are women and it is the woman who bears the human race. Perhaps God has seen our plight, and not wanting us to perish, has provided us with all this. Let us take it in good grace!"

They did. Some went for firewood. Others fetched water. They cooked and ate.

Every day they would dance the women's dance in great happiness and then sleep.

One evening a lion came in search of insects and found them dancing. But seeing such a large number of girls, he became frightened and left. Their number was such as would frighten anyone.

It then occurred to the lion to turn into a dog and go into their compound. He did. He went there looking for droppings of food. Some girls hit him and chased him away. Others said, "Don't kill him. He is a dog and dogs are friends!"

But the skeptical ones said, "What kind of dog would be in this isolated world? Where do you think he came from?"

Other girls said, "Perhaps he came all the way from the cattle-camp, following us! Perhaps he thought the whole camp was moving and so he ran after us!"

Diirawic's sister was afraid of the dog. She had not seen a dog following them. And the distance was so great that the dog could not have traveled all the way alone. She worried but said nothing. Yet she could not sleep; she stayed awake while all the others slept.

One night the lion came and knocked at the door. He had overheard the names of the older girls, one of them, Diirawic. After knocking at the door he said, "Diirawic, please open the door for me." The little girl who was awake answered, chanting:

"Achol is asleep,
Adau is asleep,

Nyankiir is asleep,
Diirawic is asleep,
The girls are asleep!''
The lion heard her and said: "Little girl, what is the matter with you,
staying up so late?''

She answered him, saying, "My dear man, it is thirst. I am suffering
from a dreadful thirst.''

"Why?'' asked the lion. "Don't the girls fetch water from the river?''

"Yes,'' answered the little girl, "they do. But since I was born, I do
not drink water from a pot or a gourd. I drink only from a container made
of reeds.''

"And don't they bring you water in such a container?'' asked the lion.

"No,'' she said. "They only bring water in pots and gourds, even
though there is a container of reeds in the house.''

"Where is that container?'' asked the lion.

"It is outside there on the platform!'' she answered.

So he took it and left to fetch water for her.

The container of reeds would not hold water. The lion spent much
time trying to fix it with clay. But when he filled it, the water washed the
clay away. The lion kept on trying until dawn. Then he returned with the
container of reeds and put it back where it was. He then rushed back to the
bush before the girls got up.

This went on for many nights. The little girl slept only during the
daytime. The girls rebuked her for this, saying: "Why do you sleep in the
daytime? Can't you sleep at night? Where do you go at night?''

She did not tell them anything. But she worried. She lost so much
weight that she became very bony.

One day Diirawic spoke to her sister and said, "Nyanaguek, my
mother's daughter, what is making you so lean? I told you to remain at
home. This is too much for a child your age! Is it your mother you are
missing? I will not allow you to make the other girls miserable. If necessary,
daughter of my mother, I will kill you.''

But Diirawic's sister would not reveal the truth. The girls went on
rebuking her but she would not tell them what she knew.

One day, she broke down and cried, and then said, "My dear sister,
Diirawic, I eat, as you see. In fact, I get plenty of food, so much that I do

not finish what I receive. But even if I did not receive enough food, I have an enduring heart. Perhaps I am able to endure more than any one of you here. What I am suffering from is something none of you has seen. Every night a lion gives me great trouble. It is just that I am a person who does not speak. That animal you thought to be a dog is a lion. I remain awake at night to protect us all and then sleep in the daytime. He comes and knocks at the door. Then he asks for you by name to open the door. I sing back to him and tell him that you are all asleep. When he wonders why I am awake, I tell him it is because I am thirsty. I explain that I only drink out of a container made of reeds and that the girls bring water only in pots and gourds. Then he goes to fetch water for me. And seeing that he cannot stop the water from flowing out of the container, he returns towards dawn and disappears, only to be back the following night. So that is what is destroying me, my dear sister. You blame me in vain."

"I have one thing to tell you," said Diirawic. "Just be calm and when he comes, do not answer. I will remain awake with you."

They agreed. Diirawic took a large spear that they had inherited from their ancestors and remained awake, close to the door. The lion came at his usual hour. He came to the door, but somehow he became afraid and jumped away without knocking. He had a feeling that something was going on.

So he left and stayed away for some time. Then he returned to the door towards dawn. He said, "Diirawic, open the door for me!" There was only silence. He repeated his request. Still there was only silence. He said, "Well! The little girl who always answered me is at last dead!"

He started to break through the door, and when he succeeded in pushing his head in, Diirawic attacked him with the large spear, forcing him back into the courtyard.

"Please, Diirawic," he pleaded, "do not kill me."

"Why not?" asked Diirawic. "What brought you here?"

"I only came in search of a sleeping-place!"

"Well, I am killing you for that," said Diirawic.

"Please allow me to be your brother," the lion continued to plead. "I will never attempt to hurt anyone again. I will go away if you don't want me here. Please!"

So Diirawic let him go. He went. But before he had gone a long way, he returned and said to the girls then gathered outside:

"I am going, but I will be back in two days with all my horned cattle."*

Then he disappeared. After two days, he came back with all his horned cattle, as he had promised. Then he addressed the girls, saying: "Here I have come. It is true that I am a lion. I want you to kill that big bull in the herd. Use its meat for taming me. If I live with you untamed, I might become wild at night and attack you. And that would be bad. So kill the bull and tame me by teasing me with the meat."

They agreed. So they fell on him and beat him so much that his fur made a storm on his back as it fell off.

They killed the bull and roasted the meat. They would bring a fat piece of meat close to his mouth, then pull it away. A puppy dog† would jump out of the saliva which dripped from the lion's mouth. They would give the puppy a fatal blow on the head. Then they would beat the lion again. Another piece of fat meat would be held close to his mouth, then pulled away, and another puppy would jump out of the falling saliva. They would give it a blow on the head and beat the lion some more. Four puppies emerged, and all four were killed.

Yet the lion's mouth streamed with a wild saliva. So they took a large quantity of streaming hot broth and poured it down his throat, clearing it of all the remaining saliva. His mouth remained wide open and sore. He could no longer eat anything. He was fed only milk, poured down his throat.

He was then released. For four months, he was nursed as a sick person. His throat continued to hurt for all this time. Then he recovered.

The girls remained for another year. It was now five years since they had left home.

The lion asked the girls why they had left their home. The girls asked him to address his questions to Diirawic, as she was their leader. So he turned to Diirawic and asked the same question.

"My brother wanted to make me his wife," explained Diirawic. "I killed him for that. I did not want to remain in a place where I had killed my own brother. So I left. I did not care about my life. I expected such dangers as finding you. If you had eaten me, it would have been no more than I expected."

* For the Dinka beliefs about horned and hornless cattle, see the footnote on page 57, *Deng and His Vicious Stepmother*.
† Although the Dinka have dogs and treat them with affection, puppies are used in folktales as symbols of wildness. Presumably they recall the image of rabid dogs.

"Well, I have now become a brother to you all," said the lion. "As an older brother, I think I should take you all back home. My cattle have since multiplied. They are yours. If you find that your land has lost its herds, these will replace them. Otherwise they will increase the cattle already there, because I have become a member of your family. Since your only brother is dead, let me be in the place of Teeng, your brother. Cool your heart and return home."

He pleaded with Diirawic for about three months. Finally she agreed, but cried a great deal. When the girls saw her cry, they all cried. They cried and cried because their leader, Diirawic, had cried.

The lion slaughtered a bull to dry their tears. They ate the meat. Then he said to them, "Let us wait for three more days, and then leave!"

They slaughtered many bulls in sacrifice to bless the territory they crossed as they returned, throwing meat away everywhere they passed. As they did so, they prayed, "This is for the animals and the birds that have helped keep us healthy for all this time without death or illness in our midst. May God direct you to share in this meat."

They had put one bull into their big house and locked the house praying, "Our dear house, we give you this bull. And you bull, if you should break the rope and get out of the house, that will be a sign of grace from the hut. If you should remain inside, then we bequeath you this hut as we leave." And they left.

All this time the people at home were in mourning. Diirawic's father never shaved his head. He left the ungroomed hair of mourning on his head and did not care about his appearance. Her mother, too, was in the same condition. She covered herself with ashes so that she looked grey.

The rest of the parents mourned, but everybody mourned especially for Diirawic. They did not care as much for their own daughters as they did for Diirawic.

The many men who had wanted to marry Diirawic also neglected themselves in mourning. Young men and girls wore only two beads.* But older people and children wore no beads at all.

All the girls came and tethered their herds a distance from the village. They all looked beautiful. Those who had been immature had grown into maturity. The older ones had now reached the peak of youth and beauty.

* For young people to be without any beads at all signifies disaster.

They had blossomed and had also become wiser and adept with words.

The little boy who was Diirawic's youngest brother had now grown up. Diirawic resembled her mother, who had been an extremely beautiful girl. Even in her old age, she still retained her beauty and her resemblance to her daughter still showed.

The little boy had never really known his sister, as he was too young when the girls left. But when he saw Diirawic in the newly arrived cattle-camp, he saw a clear resemblance to his mother. He knew that his two sisters and the other girls of the camp had disappeared. So he came and said, "Mother, I saw a girl in the cattle-camp who looks like she could be my sister, even though I do not remember my sisters."

"Child, don't you feel shame? How can you recognize people who left soon after you were born? How can you recall people long dead? This is evil magic! This is the work of an evil spirit!" She started to cry, and all the women joined her in crying.

Age-sets came running from different camps to show her sympathy. They all cried, even as they tried to console her with words.

Then came Diirawic with the girls and said, "My dear woman, permit us to shave off your mourning hair. And all of you, let us shave off your mourning hair!"

Surprised by her words, they said, "What has happened that we should shave off our mourning hair?"

Then Diirawic asked them why they were in mourning. The old woman started to cry as Diirawic spoke, and said, "My dear girl, I lost a girl like you. She died five years ago, and five years is a long time. If she had died only two or even three years ago, I might have dared to say you are my daughter. As it is, I can't. But seeing you, my dear daughter, has cooled my heart."

Diirawic spoke again, saying, "Dear Mother, every child is a daughter. As I stand in front of you, I feel as though I were your daughter. So please listen to what I say as though I were your own daughter. We have all heard of you and your famed name. We have come from a very far-off place because of you. Please allow us to shave your head. I offer five cows as a token of my request."*

* It is customary among the Dinka for sympathizers to give cattle to an aggrieved person to end the mourning.

"Daughter," said the woman, "I shall honor your request, but not because of the cows—I have no use for cattle. Night and day, I think of nothing but my lost Diirawic. Even this child you see means nothing to me compared to my lost child, Diirawic. What grieves me is that God has refused to answer my prayers. I have called upon our clan spirits and I have called upon my ancestors, and they do not listen. This I resent. I will listen to your words, my daughter. The fact that God has brought you along and put these words into your mouth is enough to convince me."

So she was shaved. Diirawic gave the woman beautiful leather skirts made from skins of animals they killed on the way. They were not from the hides of cattle, sheep, or goats. She decorated the edges of the skirts with beautiful beads and made bead designs of cattle figures on the skirts. On the bottom of the skirts, she left the beautiful natural furs of the animals.

The woman cried and Diirawic pleaded with her to wear them. She and the girls went and brought milk from their own cattle and made a feast. Diirawic's father welcomed the end of mourning. But her mother continued to cry as she saw all the festivities.

So Diirawic came to her and said, "Mother, cool your heart. I am Diirawic."

Then she shrieked with cries of joy. Everyone began to cry—old women, small girls, everyone. Even blind women dragged themselves out of their huts, feeling their way with sticks, and cried. Some people died as they cried.

Drums were taken out and for seven days, people danced with joy. Men came from distant villages, each with seven bulls to sacrifice for Diirawic. The other girls were almost abandoned. All were concerned with Diirawic.

People danced and danced. They said, "Diirawic, if God has brought you, then nothing is bad. That is what we wanted."

Then Diirawic said, "I have come back. But I have come with this man to take the place of my brother Teeng."

"Very well," agreed the people. "Now there is nothing to worry about."

There were two other Teengs. Both were sons of chiefs. Each one came forward, asking to marry Diirawic. It was decided that they should compete. Two large kraals were to be made. Each man was to fill his kraal with cattle. The kraals were built. The men began to fill them with cattle. One Teeng failed to fill his kraal. The other Teeng succeeded so well that some cattle even remained outside.

Diirawic said, "I will not marry anyone until my new brother is given four girls to be his wives. Only then shall I accept the man my people want."

People listened to her words. Then they asked her how the man became her brother. So she told the whole story from its beginning to its end.

The people agreed with her and picked four of the finest girls for her new brother. Diirawic then accepted the man who had won the competition. She was given to her husband and she continued to treat the lion-man as her full brother. She gave birth first to a son and then to a daughter. She bore twelve children. But when the thirteenth child was born, he had the characteristics of a lion. Her lion-brother had brought his family to her village and was living there when the child was born. The fields of Diirawic and her brother were next to each other. Their children played together. As they played, the small lion-child, then still a baby, would put on leather skirts and sing. When Diirawic returned, the children told her, but she dismissed what they said. "You are liars. How can such a small child do these things?"

They would explain to her that he pinched them and dug his nails into their skins and would suck blood from the wounds. Their mother simply dismissed their complaints as lies.

But the lion-brother began to wonder about the child. He said, "Does a newly born human being behave the way this child behaves?" Diirawic tried to dispel his doubts.

But one day her brother hid and saw the child dancing and singing in a way that convinced him that the child was a lion and not a human being. So he went to his sister and said, "What you bore was a lion! What shall we do?"

The woman said, "What do you mean? He is my child and should be treated as such."

"I think we should kill him," said the lion-brother.

"That is impossible," she said. "How can I allow my child to be killed? He will get used to human ways and will cease to be aggressive."

"No," continued the lion. "Let us kill him by poison if you want to be gentle with him."

"What are you talking about?" retorted his sister. "Have you forgotten that you yourself were a lion and were then tamed into a human being? Is it true that old people lose their memory?"

The boy grew up with the children. But when he reached the age of herding, he would go and bleed the children by turn and suck blood from their bodies. He would tell them not to speak, and that if they said anything to their elders, he would kill them and eat them.

The children would come home with wounds, and when asked, would say their wounds were from thorny trees.

But the lion did not believe them. He would tell them to stop lying and tell the truth, but they would not.

One day he went ahead of them and hid on top of the tree under which they usually spent the day. He saw the lion-child bleed the children and suck their blood. Right there, he speared him. The child died.

He then turned to the children and asked them why they had hidden the truth for so long. The children explained how they had been threatened by the lion-child. Then he went and explained to his sister, Diirawic, what he had done.

# Kir and Ken and
# Their Addicted Father

THIS IS AN ANCIENT EVENT.

Achol and Ayak were co-wives. They had sons called Kir and Ken. They were still small boys. Their father was a very heavy smoker. He would almost eat people if there were no tobacco.

Their father was out of tobacco. His craving for it nearly killed him. So he said, "My children, I have to sell you for tobacco!"

The children cried. When he told their mothers, their mothers were horrified. "How can you do such a thing?" they asked.

"I cannot help it," he said. "Don't you see that I am almost dying for lack of tobacco?" The wives protested, but he did not relent.

So he took the children. Ken was the smaller one, so he carried him. Kir walked. The place where tobacco could be bought was very far away. So they walked and walked and walked. The children became very tired— Kir walking and even Ken who was carried. Kir would sing to his brother, to see whether the destination was near:

> "Ken, Ken, Brother,
> Is the destination still far?"

Ken would answer:

> "Kir, Kir, Brother,
> The destination is still far."

Then Kir would continue:

> "Ken, what a hopeless land,
> The land of palms,

The land has broken my heart,
I wish we were back home!"
As Kir sang he cried. And they went on. They walked; they walked; they
walked. Then they would sing again. Kir threw himself down and cried.
Then they went on. They walked and walked, until they came close to a
large group of lions. But they were not wild. They were tamed. The
children again sang, and Kir cried.

One of the lions heard them and came towards them. The children
thought he was coming to eat them, but he was not wild; he was tamed. He
said to them, "Where are you people going?"

The man answered, saying, "We are going to the cattle-camp of the
Chief. I am going to sell my children for tobacco."

"I see," said the lion and left them.

They walked some more until they came to a forest of red trees. And
the children sang again, and Kir cried.

God saw them cry and when He saw them, He came and gave Ken a
beautifully colored stick. Neither his father nor Kir saw God give Ken the
stick. They did not even see the stick. So they walked.

The children again sang and cried and they walked on. Then they
arrived at the cattle-camp of the Lion Chief. The father was very happily
thinking about getting his tobacco. He did not care whether the lion would
decide to eat Kir and Ken or keep them as his children. All he cared about
was his tobacco.

When they arrived at the Chief's Court, the Chief asked him, "Where
are you taking the children?"

"I am a man craving tobacco; so I am here to exchange them for
tobacco."

"I see," said the Chief.

The father then put down the child he was carrying. As soon as Ken
was down, he leaped towards the Lion Chief and hit him on the head with
the stick God had given him. The Chief fell dead and all the lions dispersed
and ran away. Even the lame and the blind ran. All were saying as they ran,
"What can one do in a cattle-camp where the Chief has been killed?" Even
sleeping skins ran away. All the hornless cattle broke their ropes and turned
into lions and ran away. Each one said, "What shall I do in a cattle-camp
where the Chief has been killed?"

All the tobacco was left behind. And all the cattle with horns were left behind too.

Kir took a bull and made him a carrier. Ken took another bull and made him a carrier. Their father collected all the tobacco and walked, carrying it. The boys would not let him ride a bull. Then they began to drive all the cattle with horns toward their home.

They went back the same way; they walked; they walked; they walked.* Again they sang the song they had sung when they had come. They went for a long time, singing.

When they were near their home, Achol said, "I hear a voice like that of my Kir!"

Ayak told her, "Do not remind us of the boys, please! They are dead and forever gone!"

The mothers had thought that their children were dead. So they had shaved their heads, cut their skirts short, removed all their decorations, and covered themselves with ashes to mourn their sons.

Again, Achol insisted that the voices sounded like their children. They listened and then ran wildly towards the voices. They met the herd of cattle and wondered whose they were. "The voices," they thought, "belong to the people driving these cattle. They are not our sons' voices. Our sons are dead." But when they heard the voices again, they could not mistake them. So they ran once more until they reached them.

They met and greeted each other. Then Kir and Ken entered their home and made pegs for tethering their herd. They lived together and kept their herd together. Then they decided to divide the cattle. Their father said, "I must have my share of the cattle."

"We cannot give you a share," said the boys. "You took us there to die; you did not think we would return. So we cannot give you a share!"

When their father persisted, they hit him with the stick. He died. Then the rest of them lived happily.

---

* In Dinka, riding is expressed as "walking by bull" or "walking by horse." No distinct term for riding exists.

# Achol and Her Wild Mother

THIS IS AN ANCIENT EVENT.

Achol, Lanchichor (The Blind Beast) and Adhalchingeeny (The Exceedingly Brave One) were living with their mother. Their mother would go to fetch firewood. She gathered many pieces of wood and then put her hands behind her back and said, "O dear, who will help me lift this heavy load?"

A lion came passing by and said, "If I help you lift the load, what will you give me?"

"I will give you one hand," she said.

She gave him a hand; he helped her lift the load and she went home. Her daughter, Achol, said, "Mother, why is your hand like that?"

"My daughter, it is nothing," she answered.

Then she left again to fetch firewood. She gathered many pieces of wood and then put her hand behind her back and said, "O dear, who will now help me lift this heavy load?"

The lion came and said, "If I help you lift the load, what will you give me?"

"I will give you my other hand!" And she gave him the other hand. He lifted the load onto her head and she went home without a hand.

Her daughter saw her and said, "Mother, what has happened to your hands? You should not go to fetch firewood again! You must stop!"

But she insisted that there was nothing wrong and went to fetch firewood. Again she collected many pieces of firewood, put her arms behind her back and said, "Who will now help me lift this heavy load?"

Again the lion came and said, "If I help you lift the load, what will you give me?"

She said, "I will give you one foot!"

She gave him her foot; he helped her, and she went home.

Her daughter said, "Mother, this time, I insist that you do not go for the firewood! Why is all this happening? Why are your hands and your foot like this?"

"My daughter, it is nothing to worry about," she said. "It is my nature."

She went back to the forest another time and collected many pieces of firewood. Then she put her arms behind her back and said, "Who will now help me lift this load?"

The lion came and said, "What will you now give me?"

She said, "I will give you my other foot!"

So she gave him the other foot; he helped her, and she went home.

This time she became wild and turned into a lioness. She would not eat cooked meat; she would only have raw meat.

Achol's brothers went to the cattle-camp with their mother's relatives. So only Achol remained at home with her mother. When her mother turned wild, she went into the forest, leaving Achol alone. She would only return for a short time in the evening to look for food. Achol would prepare something for her and put it on the platform in the courtyard. Her mother would come at night and sing in a dialogue with Achol.

"Achol, Achol, where is your father?"

"My father is still in the cattle-camp!"

"And where is Lanchichor?"

"Lanchichor is still in the cattle-camp!"

"And where is Adhalchingeeny?"

"Adhalchingeeny is still in the cattle-camp!"

"And where is the food?"

"Mother, scrape the insides of our ancient gourds."

She would eat and leave. The following night, she would return and sing. Achol would reply; her mother would eat and return to the forest. This went on for a long time.

Meanwhile, Lanchichor came from the cattle-camp to visit his mother and sister. When he arrived home, he found his mother absent. He also found a large pot over the cooking fire. He wondered about these things and asked Achol, "Where is Mother gone, and why are you cooking in such a big pot?"

She replied, "I am cooking in this big pot because our mother has turned wild and is in the forest, but she comes at night for food."

"Take that pot off the fire," he said.

"I cannot," she replied. "I must cook for her."

He let her. She cooked and put the food on the platform before they went to bed. Their mother came at night and sang. Achol replied as usual. Her mother ate and left. Achol's brother got very frightened. He emptied his bowels and left the next morning.

When he was asked in the cattle-camp about the people at home, he was too embarrassed to tell the truth; so he said they were well.

Then Achol's father decided to come home to visit his wife and his daughter. He found the big pot on the fire and his wife away. When he asked Achol, she explained everything to him. He also told her to take the pot off the fire, but she would not. She put the food on the platform, and they went to bed. Achol's father told her to let him take care of the situation. Achol agreed. Her mother came and sang as usual. Achol replied. Then her mother ate. But her father was so frightened that he returned to the camp.

Then came Adhalchingeeny (The Exceedingly Brave One) and brought with him a very strong rope. He came and found Achol cooking with the large pot, and when Achol explained to him their mother's condition, he told her to take the pot off the fire, but she would not give in. He let her proceed with her usual plan. He placed the rope near the food in a way that would trap his mother when she took the food. He tied the other end to his foot.

Their mother came and sang as usual. Achol replied. As their mother went towards the food, Adhalchingeeny pulled the rope, gagged her and tied her to a pole. He then went and beat her with part of the heavy rope. He beat her and beat her and beat her. Then he gave her a piece of raw meat, and when she ate it, he beat her again. He beat her and beat her and beat her. Then he gave her two pieces of meat, one raw and one roasted. She refused the raw one and took the roasted one, saying, "My son, I have now become human, so please stop beating me."

They then reunited and lived happily.

# Duang and His Wild Wife

THIS IS AN ANCIENT EVENT.

Amou was so beautiful. She was betrothed to a man from the tribe. But she was not yet given to her betrothed. She still lived with her family.

There was a man called Duang in a neighboring village. Duang's father said to him, "My son, Duang, it is high time you married."

"Father," replied Duang, "I cannot marry; I have not yet found the girl of my heart."

"But my son," argued his father, "I want you to marry while I am alive. I may not live long enough to attend your marriage."

"I will look, Father," said Duang, "but I will marry only when I find the girl of my heart."

"Very well, my son," said his father with understanding.

They lived together until the father died. Duang did not marry. Then his mother died. He did not marry.

These deaths made him abandon himself in mourning; so he no longer took care of his appearance. His mourning hair grew long and wild. He never shaved or groomed his hair.

He was a very rich man. His cattle-byres were full of cattle, sheep and goats.

One day he left for a trip to a nearby tribe. On the way he heard the drums beating loud. He followed the sounds of the drums and found people dancing. So he stood and watched the dance.

In the dance was the girl called Amou. When she saw him standing, she left the dance and went near him. She greeted him. They stood talking.

When the relatives of the man who was betrothed to Amou saw her, they became disturbed. "Why should Amou leave the dance to greet a man who was merely watching? And then she dared to stand and talk with him! Who is the man, anyway?"

They called her and asked her. She answered, "I don't see anything wrong! I saw the man looking as though he were a stranger who needed help. So I went to greet him in case he wanted something. There is nothing more to it."

They dismissed the matter, although they were not convinced. Amou did not go back to the dance. She went and talked to the man again. She invited him to her family's home. So they left the dance and went. She seated him and gave him water. She cooked for him and served him.

The man spent two days in her house and then left and returned home.

He went and called his relatives and told them that he had found the girl of his heart. They took cattle and returned to Amou's village.

The man who had betrothed Amou had paid thirty cows. Amou's relatives sent them back and accepted Duang's cattle. The marriage was completed, and Amou was given to her husband.

She went with him and gave birth to a daughter, called Kiliingdit. Then she had a son. She and her husband lived alone with their children. Then she conceived her third child. While she was pregnant, her husband was in the cattle-camp. But when she gave birth, he came home to visit her and stay with them for the first few days after her delivery.

After she delivered, she felt a very strong craving for meat. She was still newly delivered. She said to her husband, "I am dying of craving for meat. I cannot even eat."

Her husband said to her, "If it is my cattle you have your eyes on, I will not slaughter an animal merely because of your craving! What sort of a craving is this which requires the killing of livestock.* I will not slaughter anything."

That ended the discussion. But she still suffered and could not eat or work. She would just sit there.

Her husband became impatient and embittered by her craving. He

* The Dinka kill their animals only in sacrifice, for feasts, or to honor guests. It is considered very shameful to kill a beast for meat in ordinary circumstances. However, the needs of pregnant or newly delivered women can form an exception to this general rule.

slaughtered a lamb openly so that she and the others could see it. Then he went and killed a puppy dog secretly. He roasted both the lamb and the puppy in smouldering smudge.

When they were ready he took the dog meat to his wife in her women's quarters. He grabbed his children by the hands and took them away with him to the male quarters. His wife protested, "Why are you taking the children away? Aren't they eating with me?"

He said, "I thought you said you were dying of craving. I think it would be better for you and the children if you ate separately. They will share with me."

He seated them next to him, and they ate together. She never doubted what he said, even though she felt insulted. That he would poison her was out of the question. So she ate her meat.

As soon as she ate her fill, her mouth started to drip with saliva. In a short while, she became rabid. Then she ran away, leaving her little baby behind.

Her husband took the boy to the cattle-camp and left only the girl at home. She suffered very much taking care of her baby brother. Fearing that her mother might return rabid, she took the remainder of her mother's dog meat, dried it, and stored it. She would cook a portion of it and place it on a platform outside the hut together with some other food she had prepared.

For a while, her mother did not come. Then one night, she came. She stood outside the fence of the house and sang:

> "Kiliingdit, Kiliingdit,
> Where has your father gone?"

Kiliingdit answered:

> "My father has gone to Juachnyiel,
> Mother, your meat is on the platform,
> Your food is on the platform,
> The things with which you were poisoned.
> Mother, shall we join you in the forest?
> What sort of home is this without you?"

Her mother would take the food and share it with the lions. This went on for some time.

In the meantime, the woman's brothers had not heard of her giving birth. One of them, called Bol because he was born after twins, said to the others, "Brothers, I think we should visit our sister. Maybe she has given birth and is now in some difficulties taking care of herself and the house."

The little girl continued to labor hard looking after the baby and preparing food for the mother and themselves. She also had to protect herself and the baby so their mother would not find them and having become a lioness, eat them.

She came again another night and sang. Kiliingdit replied as usual. Her mother ate and left.

In the meantime, Bol took his gourds full of milk and left for his sister's home. He arrived in the daytime. When he saw the village so quiet, he feared that something might have gone wrong. "Is our sister really at home?" he said to himself. "Perhaps what I was afraid of in my heart has occurred. Perhaps our sister died in childbirth and her husband with the children have gone away and abandoned the house!"

Another part of him said, "Don't be foolish! What has killed her? She is a newly delivered mother and is confined inside the hut."

"I see the little girl," he said to himself, "but I do not see her mother." As soon as the little girl saw him, she raced towards him, crying.

"Where is your mother, Kiliingdit?" he asked her in haste.

She told him the story of how her mother turned wild, beginning with her mother's craving for meat and her father's poisoning her with dog meat.

"When she comes in the evening," she explained, "her companions are the wives of lions."

"Will she come tonight?" asked her uncle.

"She comes every night," answered Kiliingdit, "But, Uncle, when she comes, please do not reveal yourself to her. She is no longer your sister. She is a lioness. If you reveal yourself to her, she will kill you and the loss will be ours. We shall then remain without anyone to take care of us."

"Very well," he said.

That night, she came again. She sang her usual song. Kiliingdit sang her response.

As she approached the platform to pick up her food, she said, "Kiliingdit, my daughter, why does the house smell like this? Has a human being come? Has your father returned?"

"Mother, my father has not returned. What would bring him back? Only my little brother and I are here. And were we not human beings when you left us? If you want to eat us, then do so. You will save me from all the troubles I am going through. I have suffered beyond endurance."

"My darling Kiliingdit," she said, "how can I possibly eat you? I know I have become a beast of a mother, but I have not lost my heart for you, my daughter. Is not the fact that you cook for me evidence of our continuing bond? I cannot eat you!"

When Bol heard his sister's voice, he insisted on going out to meet her, but his niece pleaded with him, saying, "Don't be deceived by her voice. She is a beast and not your sister. She will eat you!"

So he stayed; she ate and left to join the wives of the lions.

The next morning, Bol returned to the cattle-camp to tell his brothers that their sister had become a lioness. Bewildered by the news, they took their spears and came to their sister's home. They took a bull with them. They walked and walked and then arrived.

They went and sat down. The little girl went ahead and prepared the food for her mother in the usual way. Then they all went to sleep.

The little girl went into the hut with her baby brother, as usual, but the men slept outside, hiding in wait for their sister.

She came at night and sang as usual. Kiliingdit responded. She picked up her food and ate with the wives of the lions. Then she brought the dishes back.

As she put them back, she said, "Kiliingdit!"

"Yes, Mother," answered Kiliingdit.

"My dear daughter," she continued, "why does the house feel so heavy? Has your father returned?"

"Mother," said Kiliingdit, "my father has not returned. When he abandoned me with this little baby, was it his intention to return to us?"

"Kiliingdit," argued the mother, "if your father has returned, why do you hide it from me, dear daughter? Are you such a small child that you cannot understand my suffering?"

"Mother," Kiliingdit said again, "I mean what I say, my father has not come. It is I alone with the little baby. If you want to eat us, then eat us."

As the mother turned to go, her brothers jumped on her and caught her. She struggled in their hands for quite a long time, but could not break away. They tied her to a tree. The next morning, they slaughtered the bull they had brought. Then they beat her and beat her. They would tease her with raw meat by bringing it close to her mouth and pulling it away from her. Then they would continue to beat her. As she was teased with meat, saliva fell from her mouth and formed little puppies. They continued to tease her and beat her until three puppies had emerged from her saliva. Then she refused raw meat. She was given roast meat from the bull and she ate it. The brothers beat her some more until she shed all the hairs that had grown on her body.

Then she opened her eyes, looked at them closely, sat down and said, "Please hand me my little baby."

The baby was brought. He could no longer suck his mother's breasts.

When the mother had fully recovered, her brothers said, "We shall take you to our cattle-camp. You will not go to the cattle-camp of such a man again!"

But she insisted on going to her husband's cattle-camp, saying, "I must go back to him. I cannot abandon him."

Her brothers could not understand her. They wanted to attack her husband and kill him, but she argued against that. When she saw that they did not understand her, she told them that she wanted to take care of him in her own way. She was not going back to him out of love but to take revenge. So they left her and she went to her husband.

When she got to the cattle-camp, he was very pleased to have her back. She did not show any grievance at all. She stayed with him, and he was very happy with her.

One day she filled a gourd with sour milk. She pounded grain and made porridge. Then she served him, saying, "This is my first feast since I left you. I hope you give me the pleasure of finding it your heartiest meal."

First he drank the milk. Then came the porridge with ghee* and sour milk mixed into it. He ate. Then she offered him some more milk to drink on top of the porridge. When he tried to refuse, she pleaded with him. The man ate and ate and ate, until he burst and died.

---

* This Hindi term for clarified butter has gained currency among anthropologists writing about the Dinka and the Nuer. The Dinka term is *miok*.

# Nyanbol and Her
# Lioness Mother-in-law

THIS IS AN ANCIENT EVENT.

An elder had a son called Kon. He was an only child. He grew until he matured. Then his father said, "My son, it is time for you to marry!" He agreed to his father's request and was betrothed.

His mother was a lioness. When her son was married, she asked for her daughter-in-law to be brought to her house. So the son's bride was brought there and Kon's lioness-mother ate her.

Her son waited for a year and remarried. His mother again asked for his bride to be brought to her house. And again she was brought there. And his mother ate her.

That way, she finished all the girls of the area. Only one girl, called Nyanbol, remained. Kon's father asked his son to marry again, but he refused. His father insisted. Kon eventually agreed, and married her.

Five days after the marriage, his mother asked that the bride be brought to her house. The elders refused, saying she would no longer be allowed to see her son's wife. But she pleaded with them until they agreed to let the bride visit her.

The bride went with her younger sister. Kon's mother seated them. The bride's sister cooked, and they all ate.

When it was bedtime, Kon's mother suggested that her daughter-in-law share her bed with her. But Nyanbol refused. So the bride slept with her sister on one side of the hut, while the old woman slept on her bed alone on the other side.

There were many skulls in the hut, the skulls of all the women Kon's

mother had eaten. When the bride saw them she said to her mother-in-law, "Mother, what are these skulls?"

"Daughter," she said, "death has wiped out my people. As they died, I severed their heads and kept their skulls to remember them."

"I see," said the bride.

During the night, the old woman would begin to turn wild and when the bride noticed what was happening, she said, "Mother, how did all those people die?"

"They all died of disease," answered her mother-in-law.

"I see," she said.

The following day, the old woman went to hunt. While she was away, the bride's sister suggested that they leave. So they left. They ran and ran and ran.

When the old woman came and found them gone, she became enraged and ran after them. She was so wild that she made a red dust storm as she ran.

Nyanbol's little sister saw her from a distance. There was a tall palm tree nearby. The palm tree was the sacred tree of their clan. Her little sister said, "Nyanbol, you are our eldest; pray to the spirits of our clan so that this palm tree will bend for you to climb to safety."

So the elder sister prayed and said, "Palm Tree, emblem of my ancestors, you have received your share from the cattle of my marriage. Please bend so that I may get to your top."

The tree bent and she climbed onto its top. As soon as she was on top, the tree straightened up.

The younger sister decided to run ahead to take the message home. As soon as the tree straightened up, the woman arrived. The little girl had only just begun to leave. But the woman did not harm her; she said, "It is your sister I want. You may go, I will get her even from the top of that tree."

So the little girl ran ahead while the woman started to cut the tree with an axe. She cut and cut and cut, saying, "I will see to it that this palm tree falls!"

The little girl ran and ran and ran. Whenever Nyanbol saw people passing by, she sang:

> "People going to the cattle-camp,
> Please tell Kon Kerbeek,

'Kon Kerbeek, your mother has finished the daughters
of the tribe.
I alone have remained.
She is doing what she has been doing.'
O, people going to the camp,
There is no more to be said,
Nyanbol is no longer a person among the living."

Meanwhile, her sister ran and ran and ran. Eventually she arrived at the
cattle-camp and said to Kon, "Brother Kon, you will not reach your wife;
you will find her eaten by your mother!"

Kon got up and ran. When people were about to follow him, he
insisted that he go alone. He ran and ran and ran. Nyanbol sang and sang
and sang.

Then she saw him from a distance and was pleased. But she went on
singing, and Kon's mother went on cutting the tree.

Kon took his mother by surprise when he arrived. She turned to him
and said, "Kon, my son, your wife has gone to the top of this tree and I
have been begging her to come down, but she has refused. That is why I am
cutting the tree, so that I may save her."

Kon turned to his wife and said, "Pray to your emblem, the Palm Tree,
to bend, so that you may come down and we may leave."

Nyanbol prayed and the tree bent. Then they all left and returned
home to his mother's house. That night, Kon said to his mother, "I will
sleep in the cattle-byre with my wife; you sleep in the hut." He blocked
the door with heavy logs on the outside so that she could not get out, and
then set the hut on fire. Thus he killed his mother.

# Ayak and Her Lost Bridegroom

THIS IS AN ANCIENT EVENT.

Ajiech was so handsome, so very handsome. He was about the most handsome of all men.

Ajiech married a girl called Ayak. He brought the cattle for the marriage with his age-mates. Among his age-mates was a lion. But no one knew he was a lion. They drove the cattle to Ayak's family.

A very great feast was held by Ayak's family. People ate and ate. One night during the celebration, while Ajiech was in a deep sleep, the lion came and gave him some medicine so that he would not wake up from his sleep. Then he took him away to his home. He broke his neck and seated him in the hut with his back resting against the wall. Then he left the body under the care of his wife.

Meanwhile, Ayak was shaken with sudden grief. She cried and cried and cried, and wandered away from her house. She just walked and walked in the wilderness, not knowing or caring where she was going. She did not care whether she lived or died.

On the way, she met a group of foxes and sang as they approached:

"My man Ajiech,
My man, Ajiech, the Shining One,
He courted me with tenderness,
He courted me with the sweet words of youth,
The sweet words of age-mateship,
And when he married me,

He paid a hundred cows which I could not count,

O, Ajiech, my shining husband."

The foxes asked her, "Lady, what is the matter? Why are you crying?"
She answered, saying, "I have lost a man. He had just brought his
cattle for marriage, but had not yet completed the marriage, when someone
came and took him away; I do not know where he has been taken."

The foxes then consoled her and said that they had seen a person
passing by, carrying something on his shoulders. "Hurry, you may never
catch up with him; he is really a long way away."

She threw herself down, crying. Then she got up and ran on. She ran
and ran, until she met a group of lions. She sang the same song to them as
they approached. They asked her what was troubling her. When she
explained to them, they said, "We met a man on the way, carrying something on his shoulders, but if he is the one, he is too far; you can never
catch up with him."

She said to them, "Please do not kill my hope. Why do you put it that
way? I must catch up with him."

And she ran and ran and ran. Then she met a group of hyenas and
sang to them. She went on running and meeting all sorts of animals until
she met a herd of elephants. They told her they had seen a man enter a
village. One bull took pity on her and offered to carry her there. They ran
and ran until they could see houses in the distance. When the elephant
pointed out the huts, she pretended she did not see them. She wanted the
elephant to take her right into the village.

Only when they were nearly there did she agree she saw the huts.
The elephant then put her down to enter the village by herself. But the
elephant gave her some medicine and said, "This will be your weapon
against the lion. If he attacks you, throw some into his face and he will fall
dead. But then put this other medicine in his nostrils and he will come back
to life. When he comes back to life, have him remake your husband exactly
as he used to be. Make sure the lion makes him so well that he can run with
the wind. When he has made him perfect, he will probably want to kill him
again. At that point, throw the medicine in the lion's face. He will die. But
then bring him back to life again so that he may bless you in his last words."

She went and sat near the cooking-place in front of a hut and sang.
She sang until the wife of the lion came and asked her what she wanted.

"My husband is inside that hut," she said. "I want him."

"You will never have him," said the lioness.

"I have an idea," said Ayak. "You are a woman and I am a woman. Why don't you create him, make him come back to life as complete as he used to be, and then we will fight in competition for him. I dare you!"

The lioness got angry and said, "Very well, he will be created this evening."

That night, the lioness asked Ayak to kindle the fire so that she might have light to work with. As she kindled the fire, Ayak sang:

> "Fire, fire, come, light up,
> Our word is a word of honor,
> Fire, fire, come, light up,
> Our word is a word of honor."

When the fire died down, Ayak threw more grass into it and sang.

The lioness worked until Ajiech was recreated. But one eye was pulled in. So Ayak said, "My dear woman, did you not see that his eyes were perfect? Go on, make them what they used to be!"

So the lioness worked on his eyes. Then Ayak said, "He used to outrun the wind; so bring back his speed. He was also a very strong man, who could pull down a big tree. That husband of mine was not an ordinary man."

The lioness worked on him again. But when he raced with the wind, he was outrun. Ayak insisted that she work on him some more. She worked on him until he was perfect in every way.

Then the lioness said, "It is now time for us to fight for him. I cannot leave him to you!"

So they fought. After wrestling for some time, the lioness began to turn wild in order to eat her, but Ayek threw the medicine into her face. The lioness died. So Ayak put the medicine of life into her nostrils and she came back to life.

Then the lioness said, "My dear woman, I will no longer stand between you and your husband. Go with him. You will have seven children, but on the birth of your seventh child you will both die together the same day."

Ayak said, "Increase the number of children we shall have."

"Very well," said the lioness. "You will have eight children and they will all grow up to be big. But you will both die the day you bear your eighth child."

"Very well," said Ayak. "Our children will continue our life if we die."

# Ajang and His Lioness-Bride

THIS IS AN ANCIENT EVENT.

There was a man called Ajang, son of Tuong. He was so handsome, so awfully handsome! And he was his father's and mother's first-born. He had only one sister, called Ayak. They lived together at home. One day he went to the cattle-camp with his sister.

The fame of Ajang's handsomeness had penetrated the land to an awesome extent. A lioness-girl called Achol heard about him. And when she did, she left her home, saying, "I must see this Ajang, whose handsomeness is so renowned."

She travelled, catching people on the way. Whoever she caught said to her, "Even if you eat me, what does it matter? Will you have eaten Ajang? If you were to eat Ajang, that would bring disaster to our tribe, but if it is me you eat, that is not significant."

She would ask her victims, "What sort of a person is this Ajang?"

"Ajang is an extremely handsome man," she would be told. "Even in a crowded dance, he is unmistakable. If he is not in a dance, everyone feels his absence. That dance cannot succeed. So you see, I am nothing compared to Ajang."

She would eat that person and proceed. She devoured many people that way as she travelled across the country. When she was near Ajang's village, she came across a child and caught him. The child said to her, "What if you eat me? Will you have eaten Ajang?"

"What is so special about Ajang?" she asked him.

"Ajang is such a great handsome man that if he were to die, it would

III

be a disaster, but if I were to die, nothing would happen."

"Is that so?" she asked.

"Yes!" said the child.

"I will not eat you then," she said. "Just tell me where Ajang's village is."

"Ajang's village is very far; it is not near," the boy said. "You will have to walk for a long distance yet before you reach it."

"Very well," she said as she left the child and went on her way.

She walked and walked, until she found some children herding sheep and goats. She caught one of them. The boy said the same thing. "Even if you eat me, will you have eaten Ajang?"

"Where is Ajang's village?" she asked the boy.

"It is a long way ahead," the child answered.

She continued attacking children and being told the same thing for a whole day. She caught so many children that she was no longer eating them. She only talked to them and let them go. Eventually she caught another boy near Ajang's village. The boy made the same remark: "Even if you eat me, you will not have eaten Ajang."

"I will not eat you if you show me where Ajang's village is," said the lioness.

"You mean I should show you Ajang's village so that you will be able to go and eat him?"

"Of course not," replied the lioness. "I will not eat Ajang either. Can a person dare to eat such an important man, however ferocious a lioness that person may be?"

"In that case," said the boy, "there is Ajang's village, the one with that high decorated pillar."

"Wonderful," said the lioness as she hurried towards the village.

She was well received and made to sit as a guest. Ajang came and greeted her. And then he asked her, "Where do you come from?"

"I come from a very distant land," she answered.

"Where is that?" asked Ajang.

"My country is extremely far," said the lioness. "It is your fame which brought me to this country. I would like to be a lady of this house!"

"You would?" said Ajang.

"Yes, very much so," she responded.

"I don't think that can be!" Ajang said.

"Why not, when I have so much desired to be your wife?" said the lioness.

Ajang insisted, "I will not give in to your desire. It would have been better if I had seen you and then pursued you myself into that distant land of yours. That you should seek me yourself is not proper."

But the lioness continued to plead: "How can you refuse me when I have come all this way because of your fame? Please, let me be your wife."

They argued for a long time until other people intervened and persuaded Ajang, saying:

"The desire that made her leave such a far-off land must be honored. How can you even think of sending such a person away! You must have her."

Ajang surrendered.

After some time, the lioness suggested that they both go to see her relatives and then return to live in their marital home. Ajang agreed. They left at night and did not tell anybody where they were going. They walked; they walked; they walked, and they walked. Then they arrived at her home.

She had left only her mother in the house. She asked her mother to bring out a fresh set of dishes and spoons for Ajang. A special meal was prepared for him. They ate. Then they slept. They spent another day and slept again. The following night, the lioness attacked Ajang, broke his neck, and killed him. She sipped his blood and seated his body with the back resting against the wall. She did not eat any of his flesh; she only sipped the blood.

Her mother said to her, "Achol, my daughter, you know this Ajang is not an ordinary man. When his people miss him, they will come and you will be in trouble. A person does not go that far to deceive a man in order to kill him. You have made a big mistake. You should have had him live with you as your husband as you had agreed."

Achol tried to console her mother, "Everything will be all right, Mother; nothing will happen."

In the meantime, people in Ajang's village came to the conclusion that he must have been led away by Achol. So they left in a large group. They walked; they walked; they walked. After many days, they arrived at Achol's house.

On their arrival, they found Achol absent. She had gone hunting. Only her mother was at home. Ajang was still sitting dead inside the hut with his back resting against the wall.

When Achol's mother saw them, she went to greet them. But they refused, saying, "First bring us Ajang, and then come back as a friend."

Achol's mother got up and started singing to her daughter, who was still away:

"Achol, my daughter,
This is what you wanted.
O, my daughter,
I will give you a sleeping skin.
Daughter, I will give you at least a small skin.
Ajang, son of Tuong, has disappeared,
He is forever gone.
Repair him, and do it well, my daughter,
Make him be what he used to be.
Achol, now you know what comes out of evil."

At first Achol did not hear her mother's song. So her mother sang again. This time Achol heard her and rushed home. As she was approaching the house, her mother sang again. When Achol arrived, the men asked her, "Achol, have you truly come?"

"Yes," she said.

"Where is Ajang?" they asked.

"He is inside the hut," she answered.

"Is he alive or is he dead?" they asked.

"He is dead," she answered.

"Well then go into the hut and bring him back to what he used to be so that we may return with him."

She went away but did not go into the hut where Ajang was.

"Achol," said the men impatiently, "if you want a good thing and not a bad thing, you better be quick and make Ajang what he used to be! If you do not, we will leave only after killing you."

So she entered the hut and worked on Ajang. She worked and worked, until Ajang could stand. But when he emerged from the hut and tried to walk, he limped.

They said to her, "Take him back into the hut and work on him some more. When you took him away from us, he did not limp. Nor was he ugly."

So she went back and worked on him some more. When he emerged again, one eye was drawn in. They told her to make his eyes what they used to be. She went back and worked on him some more. He then emerged fully repaired.

"Ajang used to race with the wind," they said. "Make him run with the wind; let us see whether he has truly recovered his speed."

She made him run with the wind. His speed was equal to that of the wind and even greater.

"Now he is what he used to be," they said.

But they did not leave Achol after all; they killed her and her mother, and burned them in their hut.

Then they took Ajang and returned to their village. When they arrived at the village, drums were brought out and a dance was called. People danced a great deal.

Ajang's father then said, "My son is an only child; if he does not marry and something goes wrong again, he may die without leaving a child through whom I can continue to see him," So he found a girl for his son. Ajang was given his wife and they lived very happily.

# Awengok and His Lioness-Bride

THIS IS AN ANCIENT EVENT.

Awengok was so handsome, so handsome. A lioness-girl called Ayak was also famed for her beauty. When she heard of Awengok, she left her home to visit.

Awengok's home was so far that she had to travel for a very long time. Whenever she caught a child on the way, the child said, "What does it matter if you eat me? If you were to eat Awengok, that would be different, for his death would destroy our tribe!" Then she would say, "I did not catch you to eat you, I just want to know the way to the house of Awengok." The child would say, "You want me to show you his place so that you can eat him?" She would answer, "How can I eat such an important man? I just want to see him because I have heard so much about him." The child would then direct her. This went on until she arrived at Awengok's cattle-camp.

At the camp, she was met and seated with respect. Then she talked to Awengok and said, "I come from a very distant land. I am an only child, and it was not easy for me to leave my mother alone. But when I heard of your fame I decided to visit you. In my country, much is said about my beauty. So I thought I should see a man so famed for his handsomeness. It is now for you to tell me the word of your heart. If I am appealing to you, you have me. But since I left my mother alone, you and I would have to go to my home. If you don't want me, you can tell me frankly."

Awengok said, "You have come from a distant land, you are a very beautiful girl, and you are about my age. How can I refuse you?"

So they slept. The next day, they left. They walked and walked and walked until they arrived at her home. Then she said to him, "You see that thicket? That is my home. I am a lioness. I have eaten many human beings in that bush."

"I see," said Awengok. "For me, nothing has changed. Even if you are a lioness, that you thought of travelling all that distance to bring me here makes me accept you without fear. So let us proceed to your home."

They walked some more and then entered the village. She seated him in the hut and went to see her uncle. She said, "Uncle, I have brought the famous Awengok. Come let us go so that we may eat him together!"

"Why should we eat him?" remarked her uncle. "Do you consider it right to destroy such beauty just for meat? I will not take part in your plan."

"In that case," said Ayak, "keep out of this matter."

She went to her father's sister, but she too refused. She went to her mother's sister, but she too refused and said: "What evils you bring to your relatives! How can you take away from the human race such a handsome man? Don't you have respect for the Creator who made him so handsome? None of my family will join you in eating him."

She said to them, "If my family has rejected me, I do not care. Keep out of this. I will do it all by myself."

So she went. Until then, she had not raised the matter with her mother. She took it for granted that her mother would join her in killing the man. So she said to her, "Mother, all our relatives have refused to join our feast, so we will eat the man alone!"

"O no, my daughter," protested the mother. "We cannot eat him."

"Why not?" she said. "We must eat him."

"If you want to eat him," said her mother, "then go ahead alone. I will not be a part of it. I too have had children, and I know the beauty of a child. How can I deprive his people of him when he is such an extraordinary child. It is bad enough that you have brought him this far. His family must now be missing him very much. Live with him as your husband. Do not kill him."

"I brought him in order to eat him," she said. "I cannot leave him."

They left the matter there. That evening as Awengok entered the hut, Ayak jumped on him, carried him into the rear of the hut, and broke his neck. Then she seated his body with his back resting against the wall. She began to eat him. She ate and ate and ate.

Then she took the fat from inside the body and spread it outside the hut to dry. While it was drying, a dark bluebird came, picked it up and flew away with it. He carried it to the cattle-camp of Awengok. He sat with it on a pole and began to sing:

> "Man who is repairing the ropes,
> The lioness-girl says, 'What delicious flesh,
> The flesh of Awengok,
> The flesh of the son of a slim girl.' "

The man who was working on the ropes said, "Go away bird: you are making too much noise. I don't want to hear your voice."

But the bird went on singing. Some children who were standing nearby picked up stones and threw them at the bird. But the bird did not fly away. He dodged the stones and went on singing:

> "Woman who is washing the dishes,
> The lioness-girl says, 'What delicious flesh,
> The flesh of Awengok,
> The flesh of the son of a slim girl.' "

The woman said, "What is it about my dishes that the bird sings?" She went on washing her dishes. Since she did not understand what the bird was saying, she said, "Bird, will you please repeat your song." The bird agreed and sang again. The woman did not understand. She went on washing her dishes.

But a small boy heard the bird and said to his father, "Father, I think this bird is saying something important. Will you please come here so that we can hear it together. We have been ignoring him, but I think he has an important message."

His father said, "What nonsense children believe. Don't bother me with the rubbish of birds."

"Father," insisted the boy, "please come and hear him even though you do not believe I am telling the truth!"

So the father went and listened to the bird.

"You see, Father," said the boy, "that girl who took Awengok from here has eaten him. That is what the bird is saying."

"Really!" said the father and listened some more.

"Yes," said his son.

"Bird," his father said, "your message has been heard."

The bird then flew away.

The father's age-set took their spears and ran to the house of the lioness. When they arrived there, they found her away hunting. Only her mother was home.

When her mother saw them, she welcomed them, seated them on a mat, and then came to greet them, singing:

"Your names, gentlemen.
Your names!"

They replied:

"Before you greet us,
Is our Awengok here?
His absence has impoverished our land!
His absence has left us in misery!"

The lioness then sang to her daughter:

"My daughter,
Come and put him right,
To be what he used to be.
Ayak, now you know what comes out of evil!"

Ayak came running wild to attack the age-set. The people ran away in fear and returned home.

Then came the age-set called Aliab. They did what the other age-set had done and returned home, frightened by the lioness.

When the age-set called Cuor (The Vulture) saw what had happened, they ran toward Ayak's house with the senior branch of Nyangateer (The Determined Crocodile), a junior age-set—forming one big regiment. One age-set went and sat under one tree and the other went and sat under another tree.

The mother of the lioness first went to greet Cuor, and they sang in greeting. Then she went and greeted Nyangateer, and they sang in greeting. When Ayak came, attacking, they were afraid and ran back home.

Now the junior branch of Nyangateer decided to go and were joined by young boys who were not yet initiated. They all sharpened their spears and began to run.

They arrived and were seated by the old woman. Then they sang in greeting, and the young lioness came wild to attack. The age-set immediately poured spears on her, but she scorned them, saying, "Do you think that you can do what your elders could not? Do you really think you can defeat me?"

"We may not be able to defeat you," they said, "but we are determined to try."

She retreated to get wilder and then returned, flying towards them. Again they poured spears on her. Feeling the weight and the pain of the spears, she asked them to stop and said, "You have convinced me of your power. Now let me live and I will make him come back to life."

They agreed. First she called on the bird to bring the fat which he had taken away. She worked on Awengok until he was brought back to life. But she pulled one leg into the thigh so that he was one-legged. They poured more spears on her, saying, "Did you take him in that condition? Make him what he used to be or we shall kill you."

She begged for her life and worked on him some more. When she finished remaking him, the age-set tried to have him run, but he could not. He fell. They were about to attack Ayak when she pleaded for her life and promised to work on Awengok some more. She worked until he could outrun the wind. They noticed that one of his eyes was defective. So she worked on the eyes until they were perfect. Awengok immediately started to greet the people. The age-set then said to Ayak, "Our Awengok is now back to what he used to be. We have no more feud with you. You may now enter your hut and we will spray you and your hut with blessed water so that God may keep you well."

So she entered the hut. They immediately blocked the door with heavy logs on the outside so that she could not come out. Then they set the hut on fire. The whole village came running towards the fire, saying, "Let me go and share in the meat of that wanton* girl."

---

* Dinka text, *abal*, a word which means sexually loose but is often used to describe imprudent or ill-mannered behavior in women.

# Achol and Her Adoptive Lioness-Mother

THIS IS AN ANCIENT EVENT.

Achieng gave birth to two children, Maper and Achol. They had three paternal half brothers. Achol was betrothed to a man called Kwol. The family moved to the lion territory. As Achol was still small, her brother carried her.

Their half brothers were jealous of Achol's good fortune in being betrothed so young. They agreed on a plan to abandon Achol and her brother Maper in the wilderness. One evening, they secretly put some medicine in their milk. Achol and Maper fell into a heavy sleep. That night, a gourd full of milk was placed near them, and the cattle-camp moved on, leaving them behind.

Achol was the first to wake up the next morning. When she saw that they had been left behind, she cried and woke her brother up. "Maper, son of my mother, the camp has gone and we have been left behind!"

Maper woke up, looked around and said, "So our own brothers have left us! Never mind, drink your milk."

They drank some milk and then moved into a ditch made by an elephant. This provided them with shelter and protection. There they slept.

Along came a lioness looking for remains in the camp. When she saw the ditch, she looked into it and saw the children. They cried, "O, Father, we are dead—we are eaten!"

The lioness spoke and said, "My children, do not cry. I will not eat you. Are you children of human beings?"

"Yes," they said.

"Why are you here?" she asked.

"We were abandoned by our half brothers," said Maper.

"Come along with me," said the lioness. "I will look after you as my own children; I have no children of my own."

They agreed and went with her. On the way, Maper escaped and returned home. Achol remained with the lioness. They went to the lioness' house, and she looked after Achol and raised her until she became a big girl.

In the meantime, Achol's relatives were mourning her loss. The half brothers denied having played a foul trick. But Maper explained that he and his sister were left behind and found by a lioness, from whom he had escaped.

Some years later, the camp again moved to the lion territory. By this time Maper had become a grown man. One day as he and his age-mates were herding, they came to the home of the lioness. Maper did not recognize the village. The lioness had gone to hunt. Achol was there. But Maper did not recognize her.

One of the age-mates spoke to Achol, saying, "Girl, will you please give us water to drink?"

Achol said, "This is not a house where people ask for water. I see you are human beings; this place is dangerous for you!"

"We are very thirsty," they explained. "Please, let us drink."

She brought them water, and they drank. Then they left. Achol's mother, the lioness, returned, carrying an animal she had killed. She threw the animal down and sang:

> "Achol, Achol,
> Come out of the hut,
> My daughter whom I raised in plenty
> When people were gathering wild grain.
> My daughter was never vexed;
> Daughter, come out, I am here.
> My little one who was left behind,
> My little one whom I found unhurt,
> My little one whom I raised,
> Achol, my beloved one,
> Come, meet me my daughter."

They met and embraced, and then cooked for themselves and ate. Achol's mother told her: "Daughter, if human beings come, do not run away from them; be nice to them. That is how you will get married."

Maper was attracted to Achol, and that same evening he returned with a friend to court her. Achol's mother gave her a separate hut in which to entertain her age-mates. So when Maper came with his friend and asked to be accommodated, she let them into that hut. She made their beds on one side of the hut, while she herself slept on the other side.

At night, Maper's desire for Achol increased and he wanted to move over to her side of the hut. But whenever he tried to move, a lizard on the wall spoke, saying, "The man is about to violate his own sister!" So he stopped. Then he tried to move again, and a rafter on the ceiling spoke and said: "The man is about to violate his sister!" When he tried again, the grass said the same.

Maper's friend woke up and said, "Who is speaking? What are they saying?" Maper said, "I do not know and I do not understand what they mean by 'sister.'"

So they asked the girl to tell them more about who she was. Achol then told them the story of how she and her brother had been abandoned and how the lioness had found them.

"Really?" said Maper with excitement.

"Yes," said Achol.

"Then, let us leave for home. You are my sister."

Achol embraced him and cried and cried. When she became calm she told Maper and his friend that she could not leave the lioness, for the lioness had taken very good care of her. But they persuaded her to leave with them. Their camp moved on the next morning to avoid meeting the lioness.

That morning, the lioness left very early to hunt. When she returned in the evening, she sang to Achol as usual, but Achol did not reply. She repeated the song several times, and Achol did not answer. She went inside the hut and found that Achol was gone. She cried and cried and cried: "Where has my daughter gone? Has a lion eaten her or have the human beings taken her away from me?"

Then she ran, following the cattle-camp. She ran and ran and ran.

The cattle-camp arrived at the village, and Achol was hidden.

The lioness continued to run and run and run until she reached the village. She stopped outside the village and began to sing her usual song. As soon as Achol heard her voice, she jumped out of her hiding place. They ran towards one another and embraced.

Achol's father took out a bull and slaughtered it in hospitality for the lioness. The lioness said she would not go back to the forest but would rather stay among the human beings with her daughter, Achol.

Achol was married and was given to her husband. Her mother, the lioness, moved with her to her marital home. And they all lived happily together.

# Ageerpiiu and a Lion

AGEERPIIU WAS AN EXTREMELY BEAUTIFUL GIRL.
She had two brothers, but she was her parent's only daughter. The cattle-camp moved to the *toc*.\*

The girls of the cattle-camp gathered one day on the riverside, washing their gourds. A lion came and said, "Girls, I would like some water to drink!"

One small girl got up and gave him some water. He took the water and poured it away. Another girl came, and he took the water and poured it away. All the girls came and brought him water, but he poured it away. Ageerpiiu was the only exception.

Pointing at her, the lion said, "I would like water from that girl." Ageerpiiu brought water and gave it to him. Suddenly he seized her and ran away with her. Ageerpiiu managed to free herself and ran away from him. He ran after her. They ran through the *toc*, not knowing where they were going. They ran and ran and ran until nightfall. Then they arrived at a village. Ageerpiiu dropped with exhaustion in front of a hut. And the lion dropped at the edge of the village.

An elder called Ajang came out and tried to question the tired girl. But Ageerpiiu was too exhausted to speak. When the people realized that the lion was on the edge of the village, they went and killed him.

After Ageerpiiu had rested and regained her breath, she told them her story. They heard the story and said, "Do not worry, we shall take you to your family." Then Ageerpiiu and several companions left to go to her

\* A swampy grassland for dry season grazing.

home. They walked and walked and walked. They arrived in the middle of the night. First they went to the door of her mother's hut. Ageerpiiu sang:
"Mother, Mother, open the door for me!"
Her mother replied:
"Who are you?"
Ageerpiiu answered:
"It is I, Ageerpiiu."
Her mother again asked:
"With whom are you?"
Ageerpiiu said:
"I am with Nainai
And Ajak, the son of Tong."
But then her mother, not recognizing the names of the men with her, said:
"Go away, girl,
Go away,
My Ageerpiiu is long dead."
So Ageerpiiu went to her stepmother's hut and sang:
"Father's Wife, Father's Wife,
Open the door for me."
"Who are you?"
"It is I, Ageerpiiu."
"With whom are you?"
"I am with Nainai
And Ajak, the son of Tong."
"Go away, girl,
Go away,
My Ageerpiiu is long dead."
Then Ageerpiiu went to the door of the cattle-byre where her brothers slept, and she sang for them to open the door. They refused, saying their sister was dead.

Then she went to the hut of her father's junior wife. Again she sang:
"Father's Wife, Father's Wife,
Open the door for me."
"Who are you?"
"I am Ageerpiiu."
"With whom are you?"

"I am with Nainai
And Ajak, the son of Tong."
"Go away, girl,
Go away,
My Ageerpiiu is long dead."
Ageerpiiu stood bewildered, not knowing what to do. Her companions, too, were surprised. They did not know what to do. Then they heard her little half brother speaking to his mother:

"Mother, her voice sounds very much like that of Ageerpiiu! Please open the door!"

But his mother would not open the door: "Be quiet, child," she said. "Don't trouble me about Ageerpiiu, who is dead!"

"Mother," insisted the child. "Would you at least open the door and see?"

Finally she did. And she found that the child was right. Ageerpiiu and her stepmother greeted each other so much that they kept fainting. Then the other relatives were awakened. Her father, her mother, and her brothers, they all came. Her father slaughtered two bulls the same night as a sacrifice for his daughter. The following morning, he slaughtered three bulls to honor her and her companions.

Then one young man approached the family and offered to marry Ageerpiiu. But her father refused, saying: "It is now for my daughter to choose the man of her own heart. God saved her and sent her back to me, so I will marry her to whomever she wants."

Eventually she married Ajak, the son of Tong, one of the people who brought her back. Ajak released a great number of cattle for her bride-wealth. And he and Ageerpiiu were married and lived happily.

That is my story.

# Amou and the Son of God

THIS IS AN ANCIENT EVENT.

A woman gave birth to many children. Nearly all of them were boys. She had ten blind boys, ten right-handed boys, and ten left-handed boys. She had only one daughter, called Amou.

Amou did not take care of her appearance because she had to work very hard for her brothers. She would spend her days pounding grain and cooking for the family.

One summer the girls of her neighborhood assembled and said: "We had better look into Amou's problem and help her! We should make her one of us and not leave her alone with so much work. The child does not look after herself at all."

So they took her into their company. They made many beads for her. And they made her bleach her hair. Her hair turned out to be lighter than any other girl's hair in the cattle-camp.

Then came the men. They took out the drums and called a dance. The dance was attended by a Son of God. As soon as he arrived at the dance, he saw this little girl—Amou. They began to dance and soon became the center of attention. As they danced they chanted:

> "Girl, what do they call you?"
> "My dear, I am Amou."
> "Amou, you dance beautifully,
>   I am dying with the pleasure of the dance."
> "And you, what do they call you?"

"My dear, I am the Oath.*
My home is far—really far.
If it were near, I would send a person
To say, 'Father, release the cows,
Release my Grey Hornless Bull.'
And we would spend the summer in our cattle-camp
With my Hairy Pied Bull!''

As they danced and chanted, the audience gathered to watch them. People were very pleased to see a couple dance so well. They went on dancing together until the dance came to an end.

When the dance ended, the Son of God stayed with Amou. As they walked, he suggested that they go to his home. Amou agreed, and they went. When they arrived, he said to his father, "Father, I have found the wife of my heart!''

"That is wonderful,'' said his father.

Amou's people were bewildered—that she would go to a dance and elope with a man she had met for the first time. They did not even know the man who had taken her. They were very, very disturbed.

God told His Son that the girl must be returned to her family. The marriage would then be celebrated. So Amou and her bridegroom returned to her home. He went and spoke to Amou's father, saying, "It was I who eloped with your daughter. I have come back to ask you to accept me as a son-in-law. I would like your daughter to be my wife.''

Amou's father was pleased with him and said, "Your word is good. I accept.''

Then the Son of God left and said: "Let your sons make cattle pegs during the two or three days I will be away. I shall return with my cattle. When I return, I will make a storm of dust rise to announce my arrival. If you see a red storm, it is not me. If you see a brown storm, it is not me. If you see a green storm, it is not me. But if you see a blue storm, that is me.''

He left. After three days the dust storms that he had described were seen. But they were ignored. Finally, a blue storm was seen. Behind the storm was an enormous herd of cattle, including the big bull the Son of God had named in his chant.

---

* Although I do not know the precise significance of this term, it is clear that the Son of God uses it to identify or suggest his spiritual nature.

The marriage was performed. Many bulls were slaughtered for the feast. All the things that must be done in a marriage were done. Then the Son of God was given his wife. And he and Amou returned to his home in the sky.

Amou gave birth to a son. When he grew up, he said, "Mother, I would like to visit my maternal relatives."

His mother replied: "How do you know where your mother's home is?"

"Never mind how," said the child, "I know where it is."

"Wait for a little longer," said the mother. "I will take you myself when your father permits."

His father said: "If you two can find your way, you may go for a visit."

So they went. All the boy's relatives were delighted to see him. He and his mother stayed for some time, and then they returned to their home in the sky.

# Wol and Wol After a Lion's Tail

THIS IS AN ANCIENT EVENT.

A man had two sons, Wol and Wol. They were from different wives. The mother of one died soon after he was born. That boy was ill-treated by the family. He was made to sleep in the hut in which the chickens slept. In the morning he would be awakened and told to take the cattle out of the byre. Every day he was treated that way.

Then the boys' father called them and said, "My sons, I would like a tail of a lion. I would like you to get me one."

He gave his favored son a horse to travel on. And he gave his motherless son a bull. Then they left to search for a lion's tail.

The boy whose mother was dead had a married sister. On their way, the two boys decided to visit his sister and relatives-in-law. When his brother-in-law saw Wol, he asked, "Why do you travel on a bull?"

"My father gave it to me," he said. "He wants us to get him a lion's tail."

"Is that so?" remarked his brother-in-law.

"Yes," said the boy.

His sister, who was listening, offered him a horse, saying, "Why don't you take your brother-in-law's horse?"

He did and they proceeded. They walked and walked,* until they passed all the villages of the human beings. Then they entered the territory of the lions.

* In other words, they rode. See the footnote on page 93, *Kir and Ken and Their Addicted Father*.

As soon as they saw some lions, the favored son became frightened and stopped. The other Wol proceeded to the crowd of lions. He tied his horse to a tree and went to sit amidst the lions.

When the lions saw him, they thought of eating him, but the Chief of the lions said:

"He is not to be eaten yet."

He then turned to Wol and said, "Would you scratch my tail?" Wol went and scratched his tail. Suddenly he cut off the tail, jumped onto his horse and ran away. The lion's son went after him, singing:

"Wol, Wol, please return my father's tail."

Wol replied:

"I will not return your father's tail,

My father will use it for fanning the flies away!"

Wol and the lion ran and ran while they sang. When they reached the home of his married sister, Wol dropped with exhaustion in the middle of the village, while the lion dropped on the edge of the village.

When Wol took the tail to his father, his father said, "I now know which of my sons is the most worthy of my love. To you, my son who has brought me the lion's tail, I will give all my riches.

So Wol whose mother was alive and who had been the favored son turned into an unfavored son. He labored for the family, he ate only leftover food, and he suffered all the indignities the other Wol had suffered.

# Atong and Her Lion-Husband

ATONG WAS VERY BEAUTIFUL.

Many men came and offered to marry her, but she refused. She said, "I will only marry a man with a bottom lined with a string of shells." Her relatives left her free to choose her man.

A lion called Juach came and offered to marry her. Atong made her usual demand. Juach went and lined his bottom with a string of shells, then returned to ask her again. She agreed to marry him. So he paid a hundred horned cows. Then she was given to him. He took her to the lion world.

Atong had eight brothers. She also had seven sisters, she being the eighth. All together, they were sixteen. Four of her brothers advised her not to marry Juach because he was a lion. But she insisted, saying, "I want him." Her brothers finally gave in.

The lion took such care of her that she became very fat. She was not even allowed to work. When her husband saw that she was fat enough, he invited other lions to a working feast* in his fields. Not all of those who came intended to work. Many came only for the feast. The crippled, the blind, the deaf and the dumb all came. The crippled were carried. The blind were led. The deaf followed, not knowing where they were going. They all gathered and some worked in the field.

For the first time, Atong was asked to work in order to feed the guests. She pounded the grain and sieved the flour. As she worked, lizards spoke

* Among the Dinka any person may ask his neighbours, friends, or age-mates to come to a feast of meat, beer, and food to help work his field.

in the hut. "O, what a tragedy; the woman is preparing flour to be cooked with her own flesh!"

Atong did not know where the voice came from. "Who are you?" she asked. "And what are you talking about? If you are a spirit, then please let me know!"

The voice came again, saying, "Go on, do your work!"

When she resumed her work, the voice spoke again. Atong begged the voice to let her know what was happening.

The lizard then said, "It is to eat you that this feast is being held. That big pot outside is to be used for cooking your flesh!"

"What shall I do?" asked Atong. "The way out of this village goes through the field where they are working; I cannot escape."

"Stiffen one of your legs," said the lizard, "and close one eye. Also, make one arm look crippled and wear short shirts."

"Very well," Atong said.

She did as she was told. Then she left, passing near the people working in the field. Some lions saw her and said, "Oh, who is that woman? Her face resembles our dear Atong."

Atong heard them and replied in a song:

"Is your Atong this crippled?
Is your Atong one-eyed?"

Then they said, "Woman, go away. Our Atong is not deformed like you!"

She went on her way until she disappeared. As soon as she passed the fields she began to run towards her home. When it was time for her to be killed, her husband, Juach, went to the door of the hut in which she had been working and said, "Atong, come out."

The lizard spoke for her—to occupy Juach and give Atong time to escape: "Wait a little, I am still sifting the flour!"

"Very well," said Atong's husband and went away.

Then he asked her again to come out. Once more the lizard answered for her, saying, "Wait a little, I am dusting the flour off my body."

He went away and returned, asking her to come out. The lizard again spoke: "Wait a little, I am getting dressed."

Again Juach went away and returned. When he spoke, the lizard said, "Here I am in the cattle-byre."

"Well," Juach said, "come out!"

Eventually the lizard became tired and said, "Why are you bothering me? It is I, the lizard, speaking. Atong has long gone. If you are after me, then come and take me. Here I am."

So people ran after Atong. The crippled crawled. The blind knocked their heads on the trees. The deaf ran, not knowing why the others were running. Juach sang as he ran:

"Atong, Atong, wait for me.
You are a girl married with my bull,
My bull Minyiel of spreading horns.
My bull has gone to your home;
Bring him first, bring him first."

Atong replied:

"Did you marry me to be a stranger?
Son of my mother,
Was I to be a stranger?
The decorated gourd of my mother has remained in your home,
Bring it first, bring it first."

They exchanged their songs as they ran until they reached Atong's home. Atong fell unconscious in the compound, while Juach fell unconscious outside the compound.

When the people saw them, they poured cold water on Atong and poured urine on Juach. The two regained their breath.

A dog and a ram were slaughtered. The dog meat was served to Juach, and the ram meat was served to Atong. But a piece of dog meat was placed on Atong's plate. When they ate, Juach said, "Atong, why does your meat smell so nice?"

Atong responded, saying, "It is the same meat. Taste mine!" And she gave him the pieces of dog meat on her plate.

They spent many days in Atong's home. Then Juach said, "We must leave." Atong's family provided her with food and gifts. Then she and Juach left.

Four of her brothers said, "She will be eaten on the way. We had better follow them." But the other four said, "It was her own choice which took her to him. We were against her marrying him. Let her now face the danger by herself."

Eventually these brothers were persuaded by the other four, and they followed. Four walked, unnoticed, on either side of the lion and their sister.

They all walked for some time. Then the lion said, "Atong, is there nothing for me to eat?"

Atong gave him a gourd full of peanuts. He threw it down and picked up the peanuts. Then they went on.

After a while, the lion again said, "Atong, is there nothing for me to eat?"

She gave him *akop*,* and he ate it.

Then he asked again, "Is there nothing for me to eat?"

She gave him a gourd full of sesame seeds. He threw it down and picked up the seeds.

Again, "Is there nothing more for me to eat?"

In this way, he finished everything. Even the container of grain, he devoured. Nothing was left.

But he asked for more, "Is there really nothing left for me to eat?"

"All I have left is my pair of leather skirts," said Atong.

"Why don't you give me your hind leather skirt?"

Atong gave it to him.

A short while later, he said, "Would you give me your front leather skirt?"

She gave it to him.

Then they continued.

Again he asked, "Is there nothing left for me to eat?"

"No," said Atong, "absolutely nothing."

Then he said, "Well, then I must go to the top of that tree to look for fruits. You just wait for me under the tree."

He went up, and Atong waited below. He wanted to jump on her neck. As he leaped from the tree, her brothers threw their spears at him, hitting and killing him. To make sure he would not come back to life, they burned him to ashes.

They took their sister home. There they killed her and buried her.

That is the story of Atong.

* A special food prepared by breaking a paste of whole grain into tiny balls which are then fried. It can be eaten with milk, meat, fish, ground sesame, or any one of many other foodstuffs. The Dinka, the Ruweng, the Ngok, and sections of the Twic are renowned for it; it is also popular among the Shilluk, who call it *mongakelo*.

# The Four Truths

THIS IS AN ANCIENT EVENT.

A man said to his wife, "I want you to arrange my hair in four parts." The woman did as he directed. Then he went and sat under a tree and invited everybody to come and guess what each of the four parts stood for. Each person was to come with a cow-calf. The person who guessed correctly was to take all the cow-calves. He told his wife what the parts represented: "A wife is a stranger." "A half brother from a stepmother is a stranger." "A dog is a loyal friend." "A mother's brother is a loyal friend."

People came and guessed, but no one guessed correctly. Many days passed, and no one guessed correctly. All that time the man remained under the tree. He did not work at home or in his fields.

The Government decided that he was a troublemaker; they decided that he would be hanged if anyone guessed correctly. The man was guarded by four policemen armed with guns.

One day a son of his half brother said to the man's wife, "Why has Uncle abandoned his home? What is so important about this guessing game that it makes a man leave his wife and his home to sit under a tree?"

Then she said, "He is making much out of nothing. What he wants people to guess is very simple. His four truths are: 'a wife is a stranger'; 'a half brother from a stepmother is a stranger'; 'a dog is a loyal friend'; and 'a mother's brother is a loyal friend.' It is all very simple."

The boy spent the night at his uncle's home. In the morning he went and worked in the fields. Then he went and sat under the tree. People continued to guess while he listened. Eventually, he said, "Uncle, may I try?"

137

"Of course you may," said his uncle.

"Those four parts stand for: 'a wife is a stranger;' 'a half brother from a stepmother is a stranger;' 'a dog is a loyal friend;' and 'a brother of your mother is a loyal friend.'"

His uncle looked down and said nothing. "Did he guess correctly?" asked one of the policemen.

"Yes," he answered.

The man was carried away to Headquarters. The Chief said that he would be executed the following day.

The man begged the Chief, "Please do not kill me before I pay my last visit to my family! Allow me to talk to my wife before I die."

The Chief allowed him to go, guarded by four policemen. When he got to his house, he said to his wife, "My dear wife, what began as a game has destroyed me!"

"I do not want to hear anything now," she said. "Who told you to do it? Leave me alone. Go to your death."

"Won't you at least give me some milk to drink?" he begged. "I am hungry!"

"No!" she said, "I will not give you milk. Why should I waste my milk on a dying man."

So he went into the cattle-byre and cried. When the dogs saw him cry, they attacked the policemen, killing two of them. The dogs were then caught and killed.

The other two policemen took the prisoner back to the Chief. On the way, they met his half brother from a stepmother. The half brother said to him, "Brother, has that game really destroyed you? Are they really going to kill you?"

"Yes, Brother," he said, "they are going to kill me."

"If you are really going to die, then Brother, it would be a terrible waste to go with that beautiful robe you are wearing. Would you please give it to me? I will give you this one to die in."

"No!" the man said. "Keep your robe. I will die in my own robe."

So they parted and continued their separate journeys. In the meantime, the man sent word to his sister's sons, saying, "I am dying. Would at least one of you come and talk to me before I die?"

His sister had six sons. The youngest said he wanted to go alone. The eldest said he wanted to go alone. Each of the six wanted to go alone. The youngest said that unless he was allowed to go alone, he would kill himself. So he went. He ran and ran until close to dawn. When he arrived, he found his uncle had been taken to be hanged. He went to the policemen and said, "Let my uncle go; otherwise someone will die with him."

The policemen said to him, "How can we let him go when the Chief has sentenced him to death?"

"Let us go back to the Chief and discuss the matter there," he said.

When the policemen refused, the boy told them that if they proceeded with the execution they would be sure to lose one of their own.

The policemen hesitated and then decided to take the boy back to the Chief. When they got there, the boy offered to take his uncle's place and be hanged in his place: "My uncle is an only son. He has no brothers to look after his things. My mother has six sons. I am the sixth. I can die, and the five brothers will take care of our things. Please, Chief, let my uncle live."

The matter was debated and debated. Then the Chief turned to the prisoner and asked, "Why did you decide to play such a game?"

"I wanted to prove what has just happened," the man said. "I gave the secret to my wife, and she gave it away to the only person who guessed correctly. When I went to talk to her before I was to die, she rebuked me. As I was about to be taken back, my dogs attacked the policemen and killed two of them. As I came back with the remaining two policemen, I met my half brother on the way. All he cared for was my beautiful robe. And now you have just seen what my nephew has done. That is what I wanted to prove."

They saw what he meant. The Chief decided to pardon him without punishing the boy. So both the man and his nephew returned free and happy.

# Ngor and the Girls

There was a woman. She would bear a child, and the child would die. One time as the people were moving to the cattle-camp, she decided to remain at home. She had grain in plenty and ghee* filled many gourds.

A lion turned into a dog and came into her village. She cooked and gave the dog a gourd full of food. When the dog finished that, the gourd was filled again. The dog ate and then left.

He went to his fellow lions and said, "Gentlemen, there is a woman in that village who is very beautiful and very generous, but she has no children."

Ten lions decided to come and pay her a visit. When they got to her village, she cooked and gave each one of them a gourd of food and a gourd of ghee. They ate and emptied their gourds. Then they said, "May we also eat the empty gourds?"

She gave them permission to do so.

They said, "What about the gourd spoons?"

She told them to eat them too.

After they had finished eating, they said, "If there is a fresh gourd, put some water in it and bring it to us."†

She did as they asked. Each one of them spat into it.‡ Then they asked her to drink it. She did.

---

* See the footnote on page 102, *Duang and His Wild Wife*.
† Water for blessing must be in a fresh gourd which has never been used before.
‡ Spitting is used by the Dinka for blessing.

Soon after that, she conceived. When she gave birth, she had twins, one a human being, a girl, and the other a lion, a boy. The lion was aggressive from the beginning. He would pinch the other child and suck her blood. When no one was around he would climb up to the storage-place and eat the butter.

They grew up. The girl was very beautiful, and the boy was very handsome. They would go to the dances together. When they went, all the boys danced with her, and all the girls danced with him.

During the dance, he would chant:

"Twin of my mother,
Darling daughter of my mother,
We will go into thatched huts.
You will enter and I will enter.
Girls, girls,
I am a big beast with a long tail,
That is how I hold the land.
Human beings live up above;
Wol Ayong lives up above;
But we lie on the ground;
Our age-set, Marial, courts girls, *turung, turung,*
My father, Thongbeek, Thongbeek,
Is known by the children of the land.
Ayan, my bull, has grown fat.
It cannot be refused,
I am a lion who sleeps about.
Our age-set, Marial, courts girls, *turung, turung,*
My father, Thongbeek, Thongbeek,
Is known by the children of the land.
Daughter of my mother,
I drank the ghee of our mother.
Even if you insult me:
'What a hollow heart!'
The drums are loud,
The dance is hot in the bush."

Then he said, "I have got to leave because it is going to rain."
The girls said, "O, Ngor, we shall take you with us."

"But I must go now because the rain will come!" he argued.

So they all left. Women said to the girls. "Take this child of mine to watch your courtship with Ngor the lion!"

So all the children were taken along including newly born babies. Then Ngor said to the girls, "I think you should return to your homes now. I can proceed alone."

But they refused and said, "Let us spend the night in that empty cattle-byre."

So they all entered the cattle-byre. The girls suddenly fell asleep. But Ngor remained awake. He ate them all, leaving only their heads: Only the heads were found in the morning. Then he left.

He went to another dance with his sister. Again, all the men danced with his sister, and all the girls danced with him. He chanted his usual song as he danced. Again, he said he had to leave. The girls insisted on accompanying him. The children were given to them. They entered a cattle-byre. He ate all of them. Only their heads remained. Very early in the morning, he left. Word went around that Ngor the lion was a danger to the girls of the camp. So he was chased away and driven into the forest.

# Acienggaakdit
# and Acienggaakthii

There were two half sisters, Acienggaakdit (the older Acienggaak) and Acienggaakthii (the younger Acienggaak). Acienggaakdit was the daughter of the senior wife, and Acienggaakthii was the daughter of the junior wife. Acienggaakthii's mother died suddenly, so she was brought to the home of Acienggaakdit's mother. Acienggaakdit had an older sister. Her name was Ayan, but she was sometimes called by her nickname, Anyijang. She was married to a lion. Acienggaakdit and Acienggaakthii were the only girls at home.

Acienggaakdit was very proud. She saw her half sister as a useless beggar. The people at home also treated Acienggaakthii like a slave. She was sent for every errand. Achienggaakdit was no longer sent anywhere. She became the mistress of the house.

One day, the two sisters were pounding grain in a mortar with pestles. They pounded and pounded. Then Acienggaakthii put down her pestle. The pestle rolled onto Acienggaakdit's beautifully decorated gourd and broke it. When Acienggaakdit saw this, she became very angry. She wanted to fight, but was held back. She said that if she were not allowed to kill her sister, Acienggaakthii must mend her broken gourd with a hair from the tail of a lion. If Acienggaakthii failed to get the hair, she would surely kill her. Acienggaakthii was small and weak from lack of care; Acienggaakdit could easily kill her.

Acienggaakthii wondered what to do. She was her mother's only child. After her mother's death her father suddenly turned to his surviving wives and neglected her. The only person who loved her was Ayan, her half sister who was married to the lion. She scratched her head and said to herself, "What shall I do? Where shall I go?"

One day in the early hours of the morning, Acienggaakthii decided to visit Ayan. She walked and walked. When she arrived it was nightfall. But the people had not yet returned from hunting. Only her sister was at home. After she had explained her problem, Ayan advised her, saying: "Daughter of my father, when my husband comes and suggests that you two should eat together, agree; share the gourd with him. I will put two shell spoons into the gourd: a large one and a small, broken one with a hole in the center. You should take that broken spoon and use it. You will not be eating much because the food will flow out of the spoon. Nevertheless, stop eating before the gourd is empty. Leave the rest for him to finish. If you finish everything with him, he will eat you in the morning."

Acienggaakthii listened to her sister's advice. Her sister went on and said: "At night, I will cut off hairs from the tail of my husband when they begin to stand up. I will bring them to you in the hut where you will be sleeping." Her sister listened very closely and put everything into her head.

When Ayan's husband returned that evening, he said, "O, my wife, what is this that smells like a human being?"

His wife retorted: "What sort of talk is this? Have you not known all along that I am a human being? If you now want to eat me, go ahead!"

"O no!" he said, "How can I eat my wife? Where will I go if I do? Ayan, my dearest!"

He sat with doubtful heart. Once more he said, "My dear wife, there is something which smells like a human being!"

But his wife repeated: "I have always been a human being. I told you to go ahead if you want to eat me."

Then he said, "O no! How can a man eat his wife? Where would he then go? My dearest!"

Again he sat with a doubtful heart. Then he said again, "O, O, how you smell! You are more of a human being tonight than you have ever been!"

"Well," said Ayan, "if you feel like eating me, why don't you! I have always been a human being!"

He went into the cattle-byre where his sister-in-law was sleeping. As he entered, the human smell became stronger. "Who is here?" he said.

"Brother-in-law," answered Acienggaakthii, "it is I, Acienggaakthii. I have been here for some time!" She spoke very courteously as she went towards him. She was a very courteous girl. He returned to his wife and said, "How dare you hide my beloved sister-in-law from me? What have you done to make her comfortable? Serve us our dinner together; I would like to eat with her."

Acienggaakthii said, "Yes, my brother-in-law; let us eat together. How could I eat alone, having come all the way to see you?"

The lion was very pleased with her. A large meal was prepared from the meat he had brought. Then they were served. The broth was brought separately. They were given spoons for the broth. The spoons were placed in such a way that the large spoon lay in front of Acienggaakthii and the small, broken one in front of the lion. Acienggaakthii immediately remarked, "Brother-in-law, this is your spoon," referring to the larger one.

"No, no," he said, "it is yours, my sister-in-law."

"No, it is yours, my brother-in-law," Acienggaakthii insisted.

They argued and argued until the lion gave in. He took the spoon as he said to his wife, "What a lovely sister-in-law I have! She is *the* sister-in-law. I knew it from the time I married you!"

So they ate. In a short while, Acienggaakthii stopped eating. "My brother-in-law, I have had enough!"

"Sister-in-law," he said, "how can you do such a thing? How can you stop eating so soon? You are insulting me! Please eat some more!"

"No, my brother-in-law," she said, "it is just that I have had enough! There is nothing wrong!"

He understood and continued to eat. He finished the broth and continued with the meat. He ate all the meat.

Then came the porridge. There were again two spoons: a small, broken spoon and a large, hollow spoon. Again, Acienggaakthii took the small spoon and insisted that the lion take the large spoon. They ate, and when they reached the middle of the course, she stopped. The lion said to himself: "What a small eater my sister-in-law is! She is truly my favorite sister-in-law!"

Then came the time to sleep. Ayan prepared their sleeping places. Acienggaakthii slept in the cattle-byre amidst the herd. The lion slept in the hut with his wife.

The people then went to sleep. Acienggaakthii had behaved very well and her brother-in-law the lion was very happy with her. She was definitely his favorite sister-in-law. He slept soundly.

His tail began to stand up. While he was sleeping his wife cut many hairs from his tail; she wrapped them and went into the cattle-byre where her half sister was sleeping. She tied them around Acienggaakthii's arm. She told her to leave early in the morning before her husband woke up. Then she returned to her hut. Her half sister left as she had advised. Her husband woke up and went straight to hunt. He wanted to see his sister-in-law before leaving, but Ayan told him that the girl was still sleeping and should not be disturbed. "Yes, my dear," said the lion as he left, "I will go to hunt some meat for her. I will see her later."

The girl ran and ran. She came across the beautiful and delicious red fruit called *milat*, but she did not stop; she continued to run and refused to stop for any pleasures.

Kur, the small stone with which spears are sharpened, had been awake in the cattle-byre and had seen everything that had gone on. When the cattle-byre was opened in the morning for the cattle to be taken out, Kur also came out. He went into the hut of the lion and found him gone. So he decided to follow Acienggaakthii's footsteps. He ran and ran and ran, until he caught up with Acienggaakthii; then he sang, praising the lion, calling him by his bull-name, "Ebony Tree."

"Ebony Tree, Ebony Tree,
Your wife, Anyijang (Ayan),
She plucked your tail last night
And tied the hairs on her sister's arm."

Acienggaakthii responded in a song:

"What a liar of a stone you are!
Yours is not the courtesy of an in-law!
Yours is not the courtesy of the Ebony Tree!
No, it is not the courtesy of the Ebony Tree."

They continued to run. Then he sang again and she replied.

Eventually, the lions heard them singing and came running. The lions ran very swiftly until they found the stone, covered with sweat, but still running. They all joined in and ran after the girl. They ran and ran and ran. But the girl outran them.

She reached her home. When the house was quite near, all the lions returned except her brother-in-law. He went on after her until she was close to the village. The lion then stopped, but she continued running until she dropped at the edge of the village. Blood flowed from her mouth.

Neighbors saw her a distance away as she was running. When she fell to the ground, they ran and poured cold water over her. She slowly came awake. By this time her family had arrived, and she was taken home.

She mended the broken gourd of Acienggaakdit with the tail hairs of the lion.

Acienggaakdit was very disturbed by her sister's return. She had never expected her to get the hairs of a lion. "Where did you get them?" she asked Acienggaakthii. "You got hairs from a lion! I cannot believe it."

Acienggaakthii said to her, "I got them from the home of our sister. But it is a dangerous place."

They continued to work at home as before. One day as they were pounding grain, Acienggaakdit deliberately dropped her pestle and broke Acienggaakthii's gourd. Acienggaakdit pretended to be very upset by what she had done. Acienggaakthii told her not to mind, but she continued to appear concerned.

Then she said, "Since I asked you to mend my gourd with a lion's hair, it is only fair that I, too, mend your gourd with a lion's hair. So I must go to fetch the hair as you did."

Acienggaakthii tried to persuade her against doing that: "Daughter of my father, never mind my broken gourd. If you want to mend it, use a thread. You should not go to that lion home. It is an extremely dangerous place."

Acienggaakdit became offended: "Do you mean to say that *I*, Acienggaakdit, cannot do what *you*, a miserable orphan, could do? If you had to mend my gourd with a lion's hair, I, too, must. If you could get the hair from a lion, I, too, can."

Acienggaakthii suggested that if all she cared about was to mend the gourd with a lion's hair, then she could use the remaining hairs that she had brought. "Daughter of my father," Acienggaakthii pleaded, "you will be eaten. Please listen to me and use a thread or my remaining hairs."

But Acienggaakdit could not be persuaded: "Why are you so worried about me? If you went to the lion world, why should I not go? Is it perhaps because you do not want me to prove that I, too, can do what you did? Stop advising me and be silent!"

Acienggaakthii eventually gave up and said, "Do it your way, daughter of my father. I hope all goes well for you."

Early the next day, Acienggaakdit left. Eager to reach her sister's home, she ran and ran and arrived there within a short time.

She explained her problem to her sister. Her sister told her how to behave if they were to get the hairs. Her sister planned everything in the way she had planned for Acienggaakthii.

Acienggaakdit's brother-in-law returned from his hunting. Ayan wanted her sister to hide for a while so she could observe the mood of her husband. The girl hid. As soon as the lion arrived, he raised his nose towards the sky and said, "There is something here which smells like human flesh!"

Before Ayan could answer her husband, Acienggaakdit spoke from where she had been hiding: "Brother-in-law, it is I smelling that way. I came some time ago, but Anyijang insists on my hiding here: I don't know why!"

Her brother-in-law did not like her manner. He roared, saying, "My sister-in-law is broad, broad, as broad as the mouth of a spoon!"

Acienggaakdit responded with anger, "Brother-in-law, why are you insulting me? I, too, can insult you." Then she went on to say, "I have a brother-in-law with a bottom as red as the fire of the summer camp."

They exchanged a few insults and the lion became more annoyed by her presence.

Then dinner was served. Meat was brought first with broth. Acienggaakdit took the large spoon and started eating the broth while her brother-in-law, with the broken spoon, could not get any. When she finished the broth, she ate the meat as her brother-in-law watched, amazed by her greed. But she did not care. She even looked directly at her brother-in-law and said, "Am I not beautiful?"

Then they waited for the porridge course. When it came, she again grabbed the good spoon and cut through the porridge so fast that her brother-in-law decided to stop eating. She continued to eat. Her brother-in-law sat and growled as he watched her eat.

When they went to sleep, the lion remained half awake, suspicious that his sister-in-law was planning to do something.

The girl was sleeping in the cattle-byre. There were cattle in the byre. When Acienggaakthii had slept there, the cattle had trampled over her purposely. She would only say, "What soft feet the cattle of my brother-in-law have! How nice their bodies feel!" But when the cattle trampled over Acienggaakdit, she got angry: "Curse you cows!" And she took a large stick to beat them away from her, complaining, "What a stinking cattle-byre!" The animals groaned and returned to their places.

When the lion finally went to sleep, Ayan cut off some hairs from his tail. She went to the byre and tied them on Acienggaakdit's arm.

Very early in the morning, Acienggaakdit left, according to the plan. Kur, the stone, followed her, as he had followed Acienggaakthii, and he sang the same song:

"Ebony Tree, Ebony Tree,
Your wife, Anyijang (Ayan),
She plucked your tail last night
And tied the hairs on her sister's arm."

Acienggaakdit stopped and said, "What a beautiful song! Please let me hear some more!"

The stone sang the song again. Acienggaakdit waited for the stone, picked him up, and praised him, "What a wonderful voice you have!"

She carried the stone; the stone continued to sing. Then they saw the *milat* fruit. She stopped and picked some. She picked here, she picked there, she picked here, she picked there. She did not know that the lions had heard the stone sing and were already on their way, following her. The stone continued to sing.

Eventually the lions caught up with her. Before any other lion could, her brother-in-law jumped from a long distance and fell onto her neck. He ripped off her head. The head started to run, dodging the lions and heading towards the home of Acienggaakdit. It ran and ran and ran. The lions got tired of following the head. They all held their tails straight up as they ran after the head, but with no success. The head outran all the lions.

The head continued to run until it suddenly entered a hut where people were gathered. Acienggaakdit's mother was there. When the people recognized the head, they cried, "O! Acienggaakdit has been eaten by the lions!"

They addressed the head and said, "Acienggaakdit, you see why you were advised not to go! O, Acienggaakdit, if only you had listened!"

At that moment her father interrupted and said, "Bury her, she was killed by her own head." The head was buried. That is how Acienggaakdit died. She was killed by her own head.

# Thaama and Mohammed

THIS IS AN ANCIENT EVENT.

A story which used to be told in the ancient past when people played by telling stories.

A girl called Thaama was so beautiful. She was a girl of great wit and many tricks. Men came in large numbers to woo her because she was such a beautiful girl. When men came, she accommodated them, but let them sleep with her female slave. Only the slave conversed with the men.

Her fame reached every man; not a single one did not hear of her. Each man came from a far-off place, bragging that she would not resist him. He would come and call on her. She would entertain him and keep him company. When night came, the time for them to go into a hut to converse, she would send her slave into the hut to converse with the man.

A man called Mohammed, who was a judge, heard of her fame and how difficult she was to procure. Mohammed boasted, saying, "Would she ever dare do to me what she does to other people?"

One person said to Mohammed, "I think she would do it to you, too. She will keep you company in the evening. But after she has deceived you into thinking that she is interested in you, she will send you her slave to converse with you at night."

"I do not believe it," said Mohammed.

They argued until Mohammed felt challenged to prove himself. So he left to visit Thaama. Thaama received him and entertained him very well. They sat and conversed. They conversed and conversed and conversed. Then Thaama accepted his proposition to continue the conversation in a hut. She went with him into the hut. They continued to converse until Mohammed fell asleep. As soon as Mohammed was asleep, Thaama left the hut and brought her slave to sleep with him. Early in the morning the slave got up and left the hut.

When Mohammed woke up, he got onto his horse and displayed himself in the village, proud that he had had Thaama, the most difficult girl to procure. Then he returned to his territory.

He went and boasted, saying, "I have slept with the girl who was said to be impossible to have!"

"You are telling a lie," people said to him.

The matter was debated and debated. Then some people were sent to Thaama's village to inquire into the matter.

Thaama told the people that it was her slave who conversed with Mohammed and not herself.

"That is what we thought," they said.

When Mohammed heard this, he was very hurt. But he decided he would marry Thaama. So he offered a large number of cattle to her family. He paid an enormous number of cattle for her, and she was married to him. She went to his home.

When they got there, Mohammed handed her over to his slave, saying, "It was for this slave that I married you and not for myself."

"Nothing is bad," she said. "If you went and married me for your slave, so be it. I can also love a slave."

They stayed. Thaama talked to the slave and said: "I come from a very big family. At home we, too, have slaves. So please, even though I have been given to you, I beg you to respect me. Sleep alone on one side of the hut, and I will sleep on the other side."

The slave agreed and slept alone on his side. Thaama slept on the other side.

They spent three years that way. The slave slept on one side of the hut and Thaama slept on the other side.

Then she went for a visit to her family. When she came back she brought with her some beautifully decorated plates. There were four of them. They were rare and very beautiful.

Mohammed's wife saw the plates and liked them very much. She begged Thaama to give her one plate, but Thaama refused, saying, "I cannot give any one of them to you. But if you really want them, I shall give you some if you exchange beds for a night; you come and sleep in my hut and I will go to sleep in yours.''

Mohammed's wife heard her and said, "But if that is the only condition, it is quite simple. I shall go into your hut this very night. And you come into mine.''

Thaama gave her two plates and kept two plates for herself.

They did as they had agreed. Mohammed did not know. He thought he was sleeping with his wife. Only the slave knew, but he did not tell Mohammed.

That night both women became pregnant. Mohammed's wife became pregnant with the child of the slave, and Thaama became pregnant with Mohammed's child.

The next morning, their men went away on a long trek. They were away for three years on an official journey.

In the meantime, the women went through their pregnancy and bore boys. The boys grew up until they could walk.

Thaama's child, the son of Mohammed, was very brown and was a very handsome boy. The son of Mohammed's wife, on the other hand, was very black; he was the son of the slave.

When the men returned from their long journey, the women went to meet them. Thaama went and caught the reins of the slave's horse, the horse of her husband. Mohammed's wife went and caught the horse of her husband. Their children were with them. Mohammed's wife's son was very black—he was the child of the slave; Thaama's son was very brown—he was the son of Mohammed.

Mohammed's heart was in doubt. "How could Thaama have a child who looked like him while his own wife had such a black child," he wondered.

Whenever the children came to the two men, the son of Thaama would run to Mohammed, his father, while the son of Mohammed's wife would run to his slave-father.

Mohammed continued to wonder. One day, he asked Thaama, "Where did you get this child? Why does he resemble me so much?''

"When you came to marry me," said Thaama, "you found me in an important family. You saw my father was a chief. You saw that we had our own slaves. You found me an important person in my own right. Then you brought me here and dared to give me to your slave! So I tricked your wife. I bribed her with my plates to sleep with the slave and allow me to sleep with you. She accepted. That is how I became pregnant with your child and your wife became pregnant with a slave-child."

Mohammed listened very closely. Then he said, "Very well." He called his wife and said to her, "Since you wanted the slave, he will be your husband. I will now attend to this wife of mine, Thaama."

So he took Thaama and made her his wife.

That is it; my story is ended.

# TALES IN CONTEXT

In my introduction, I discussed some general literary and philosophical characteristics of Dinka folktales without going into the social and moral particulars of the tales. With this further commentary, I propose to relate the content of the tales to various aspects of Dinka life, including social structure (here treated under identification), fundamental values, flirtation and courtship, formalities of marriage, the family and kinship, power and leadership, and social change. In focussing on these aspects of Dinka life, I have been guided by the methodology followed in my earlier books.*

## SOCIAL AND MORAL IDENTIFICATION

One of the outstanding characteristics of Dinka folktales is their concern with family relationships. Dinka society is a family-oriented society. The family is the backbone around which the social structure is shaped. Families form lineages and clans, the latter being unorganized though exogamous units, sometimes spreading across political boundaries. On the political level of the territory, these lineages form sections, which in turn form subtribes; and the subtribes form the tribes. A class dimension is also provided by the family, since descent groups are divided into chiefly lineages, from which all chiefs descend, and the lineages of the commoners, who ordinarily wield no political power. Territorial political organizations are reinforced by the age-sets, which every Dinka joins on reaching the age of majority, usually in the later teens.

But the family does more than give the social structure its shape; it also lays down the ground rules which govern relationships both within the family and in the wider social circles of the Dinka.

* See Deng, *Tradition and Modernization: A Challenge for Law Among the Dinka of the Sudan*, New Haven: Yale University Press (1971); *The Dinka of the Sudan*, New York: Holt, Rinehart, and Winston (1972); and *The Dinka and Their Songs*, Oxford: The Press (1973).

Dinka folktales do not generally distinguish between the various tribes and subtribes of Dinka society; nor do they refer to people by ethnic designation, as Nuer, Shilluk, Jur, Arab, European, etc. But they often speak of the "cattle-hearth" and the "cattle-camp," concepts which are used to refer to various descent and territorial units, from the lineage to the largest corporate, territorial entities. In view of the descent orientation of Dinka society, the family or situations which prefigure its establishment—dance, courtship, marriage—often provide the scene of the stories. But symbols of other kinds of identification, notably age-sets and chiefs are occasionally encountered. Beyond the tribe, identification is unclear.

It should be remembered that the basic values of the Dinka, which concern agnatic continuity, are both group- and individual-oriented. This in part explains the system of segmentation for which the Nilotics are well known by anthropologists. Being an insider or an outsider is relative and changes according to context. Anyone who is not a member of a particular family is an outsider to that family, but within the lineage or the clan, he may be an insider; anyone who is not a member of a particular section is an outsider, but within the subtribe or the tribe, he may be an insider. However, the possibility of identification with wider circles tends to narrow as one goes farther away from the family. Until recently, when modern conditions have made them more aware of their various branches, some Dinka tribes not only considered a number of other Dinka tribes non-Dinka but feared them as cannibalistic. Some non-Dinka southern tribes were identified by such terms as *Nyamnyam*, a name which suggested that they were man-eaters.

Dinka bedtime stories tend to convey a close association between outsiders and animals, notably lions. There is as yet no sufficient evidence for firm generalizations, and one might discuss the significance of animals in Dinka stories simply from the standpoint of ecological interdependences. However, enough evidence does exist to indicate a moral classification based on a man/animal dichotomy. The characteristics which are attributed to animals are so far interchangeable with human characteristics that a lion is often mistaken for a man or woman until its aggression or other animal instincts begin to manifest themselves. Likewise, human beings begin to acquire animal tendencies in a manner that is not always said to alter their basic physical appearance. The process by which animal characteristics emerge sometimes includes reference to the animal's tail or fur, but often the process is simply described as "turning wild."Lions nearly always have human names and may even have the metaphoric ox-names which are given to men on the basis of the colors of their favorite oxen.

A person who violates fundamental precepts of the Dinka moral code is often identified in the folktales as an outsider and an animal. A tale may introduce such a person as an animal or may depict the transformation of a human being into an animal as the result of a moral violation. Within the animal world, of course, there are vicious animals and gentle ones. Vicious animals and moral derelicts who turn into vicious animals are usually killed, but some animals may be subjected to severe, ritual beating and restored to human status.

The moral identification of social offenders as animals seems clear in *Kir and Ken and Their Addicted Father*. So addicted to tobacco was the father that "he would almost eat people if there were no tobacco." By linking a craving for tobacco with a desire to eat people, the tale symbolically dramatizes the abnormalities which distinguish an animal from a responsible person. That the lions of the stories are not really lions but condemned human beings is also obvious, since men and women are often presented as having married lions, sometimes through the normal procedures of the Dinka. If they were meant to be truly lions, such mixed animal-human marriages would call for more explanations than are provided. It is, of course, the deviant who marry lions. Morally acceptable people marry human beings, and the exceptionally virtuous may even marry into the family of God. Even in their everyday language, the Dinka refer to greedy people or those who unscrupulously receive more than they give as "lions." Such moral characterization is therefore not encountered only in the realm of folktales.

If a Dinka who violates the code is seen as an animal, it is easy to understand how foreign aggressors could even more readily be identified as animals. The Dinka have been in contact with other people for centuries and witnessed waves of invaders during the nineteenth century; yet the tales do not refer to strangers by any ethnic, racial, or national terms. Out of over sixty tales examined, only *Thaama and Mohammed*, which was recorded in town, mentions a non-Dinka name, in this case, an Arab name. This story seems to reflect some of the more recent social problems resulting from intensive contacts with the outside world. Rather than disproving the thesis that Arabs and other foreigners who came into Dinkaland as slavers and aggressors were categorized as animals, the story shows the degree to which less disruptive and more intensive contacts with outsiders have now influenced the Dinka to consider those outsiders "human."

It is easy to see how *Kir and Ken and Their Addicted Father* could have originated from the circumstances of slavery, which might have tempted some parents to sell their children to invaders, either to maintain the rest of the family in the famines which often resulted from the ravages of slave-raiding or to meet less noble ends. The camp of the lions to which the addicted father took his children held bulls which had been trained as animals of burden, a non-Dinka practice which exists among the Baggara Arabs. To assume that these lions represent foreign slave traders seems reasonable.

Whether the tales envisage a social context wider than the Dinka world or not, they do embody notions of Dinka social organization, and they present the family as the fundamental unit in which the values of the Dinka find their roots; adherence to these values largely determines the identification of a person as Dinka and a desirable member of society.

## FUNDAMENTAL VALUES

The family being thus fundamental to the social order and moral identity, it is not surprising that the main goal of a Dinka is to marry and beget children "to stand his head upright." Every Dinka fears dying before securing this avenue to immortality. Dinka religion promises no heaven after death, only continuity through the living, (though another form of continued existence is given some recognition). Procreational immortality can be achieved by adoption or by the institutions of levirate and ghost marriages, whereby a man co-habits with a junior widow of his father or other relative to beget children to the name of the dead man, or marries a wife for the dead man and begets children with that woman to the name of the dead man. But procreation is best enjoyed through one's own biological children. And the more one's children, the greater the opportunity for perpetuating the qualities that are associated with the father. Among many children may be brave men, men of wisdom, and men of physical beauty. Large numbers of children are achieved through polygyny, though not all Dinka can afford to marry many wives.

While both men and women feel the desire for children, immortality through them is male-oriented. It is the sons who will continue the name of the father and all his agnatic ascendants. Daughters keep close ties with their agnatic group, but their main function is to get married and bring bridewealth cattle to their families to be used by their male relatives for their marriages. Thus, procreation lays the foundation of Dinka social stratification; for after giving prominence to the over-all life-giver and -taker, God, it honors other deities and the ancestors, whose representatives on earth are the heads of the families, to whom the women and younger generations in turn are subordinated.

This formula does not always work consistently, for women and youth have a much greater influence than the principle of procreation would ascribe. Youth tend to resort to excessive violence and aggressiveness as a means of exerting influence. Women tend to exert their influence subtly and are, therefore, more effective. This is why Dinka society is obsessed with repressing their influence. In the case of both women and youth, roles are prescribed in which they are subordinate, but they assert stronger roles in reaction. This contradiction in role creates tensions which can undermine the fundamental values of society as formulated by male elders. But eliminating the disruptive force in turn requires more controls than the system can adequately provide; hence, the paradoxical impact of women and children. These paradoxes pervade all aspects of the Dinka social process.

While agnatic continuity supports the collective interest of the group —which identifies itself with a principal ancestor—it can also engender essentially individualistic interests. Each son wants to found his own family with a woman of his own choice. His choice may not always agree with that of his father or group, and the mere fact that a son wants to start a family of his own implies a degree of independence which qualifies the role of the father whom the son is supposed to immortalize. This, combined with the interest of the women in asserting themselves, usually by influencing men against men, makes the principle of immortality through children paradoxically conducive both to group solidarity and to the kind of intragroup tensions which result in conflicts and occasionally in disaffiliation.

Marriage as a value and the individual-group tensions it engenders are the subject matter of many folktales, in which the group urges the member to marry and the member refuses. In *Chol and His Baby-Bride*, Chol's father kept pleading with him, "Son, please marry. You will disappear childless and perish forever." When Chol could not be persuaded to marry, but on the contrary took up what was seen as an odd role for a man, taking care of a newly born baby, his father said, "He is no longer of use to me. There is nothing I can do. I will give my cattle away. If it is God's will that my lineage should perish, so be it."

The value Chol's father places on children is reiterated in other tales. In *Ajang and His Lioness-Bride*, Ajang's father, concerned with the future safety of his son, who had just been rescued from a lioness, said, "My son is an only child; if he does not marry and something goes wrong again, he may die without leaving a child through whom I can continue to see him." So he procured a wife for his son, probably earlier than he would have under ordinary circumstances. In *Ayak and Her Lost Bridegroom*, when Ayak eventually defeated the lioness who had been harboring her groom, the lioness surrendered and blessed Ayak and her husband, saying, "My dear woman, I will no longer stand between you and your husband. Go with him. You will have seven children, but on the birth of your seventh child you will both die together the same day." Although the lioness agreed to increase the number of children to eight at Ayak's urging, she did not remove the threat of death. Ayak then said only, "Very well. Our children will continue our life if we die."

The conflict between the family's eagerness for marriages and procreation and the individual's reluctance to marry until he finds the girl of his choice recurs in many stories. The individual-group controversy over the timing of marriage indicates that the individual and group interests involved in agnatic continuity are not always harmonious—Chol's answer to his father's plea was: "I do not want to marry. I have not yet found the girl of my heart. When I find her, I shall marry."—Indeed, as *Aluel and Her Loving Father* shows, opposed interests in agnatic continuity may conflict so strongly that a son will kill his father or the father his son.

One of the reasons for delayed marriage is the Dinka desire to have children from a well-chosen woman. It is, at least in part, the importance the Dinka attach to heredity which made Chol choose a baby for his bride, both because of her background and because he wanted to raise her to his own liking. The point is also illustrated in *Agany and His Search for a Wife*. Although his father urged him to marry, Agany refused on the grounds that he had not yet found the girl of his heart. He made himself look so repulsive that the girls he talked to ridiculed him and sent him away, until he met Aluat, a little girl who sympathized with him and showed him unusual kindness. She he eventually married.

Connected with the idea of procuring an ideal wife to beget children is the desire for a wife who will observe the code of ideal human relations, particularly in kinship relationships. This is especially necessary because polygyny nearly always entails half kin and stepkin relationships, whether in the immediate family, the extended family, or even the fictionally extended family—the tribe. To guard against the tensions engendered in such relationships, the society postulates the goal of *cieng*, a concept of ideal human relationships designed to foster harmony and mutual cooperation among group members. These values are supposed to extend to broadened circles, but they focus on the family and weaken with distance from the family. And even within the family, the fact that society has emphasized these values to combat disharmony without uprooting its cause means that a "pretentious" conformity is achieved while tensions and even open conflicts remain engrained. This is why the theme of the jealous stepmother is so pervasive. The stepmother, not only the mother of children other than her own but the one who brings up children to observe or violate social norms, is thus envisaged as a crucial figure, potentially destructive if not well contained.

Given the manner in which the values of agnatic descent stratify people according to sex and age, the degree to which the system achieves conformity to its basic precepts is striking, despite the recurrent dramatization of nonconformity in the tales. This conformity might not be achieved if Dinka culture were not remarkable in the way it provides avenues to a high sense of dignity—even when the foundation must be largely one of vanity. The forms of dignity the Dinka recognize are subsumed in the word *dheeng*, the adjective of which is *adheng*. Among its many meanings as a noun are nobility, beauty, handsomeness, elegance, charm, grace, gentleness, hospitality, generosity, good manners, discretion, and kindness. Singing and dancing, except in prayer or on certain religious occasions, are *dheeng*. Personal decoration, initiation ceremonies, celebration of marriages, the display of oxen, indeed any demonstration of an aesthetic value, is considered *dheeng*. The social background of a person, his physical appearance, the way he walks, talks, eats, or dresses, and the way he behaves towards his fellow men are all important factors in determining his *dheeng*.

In this set of meanings one can discern at least three kinds of *dheeng*—dignity, in other words. The first is the status people achieve through material resources and social responsiveness, measured not only in terms of generosity and hospitality but also by personal integrity and responsible conduct towards others. The second kind derives from birth or marriage into a family with already established status. The third is more sensual in nature and stems from physical attractiveness and various forms of aesthetic display. The first type of *dheeng* is the norm, and its achievement is expected primarily of elders and established adults. Women and youth preoccupy themselves with the second and the third. Women pride themselves on being wives and mothers while youth, especially males, pride themselves on being the descendants of a particular line. Women and children brag a great deal, especially in songs, about being the wives or the progeny of a particular person or family line. A Dinka wife will refer to her husband interchangeably as "he" or "I," thereby identifying herself with him and enjoying his dignity by proxy. A father or a mother is designated by the name of the first-born as "father" or "mother of . . . ." This name carries with it both respect and intimacy. So important is family affiliation that to be a divorced woman or to be a widow or orphan (a status which the Dinka extend to adults) is to be miserably deprived and even degraded.

But it is self-adornment and the aesthetic which most preoccupy youth and women as a way of enhancing status and dignity. These comprise a whole range of concerns and activities. Natural beauty or handsomeness is a great blessing. To be physically complete in the sense that one is without an obvious defect is so essential that to be lame, blind, or deaf, or in any way deformed, is to be plunged into an indignity that only the most unusual person can adequately compensate for. Social consciousness dictates that handicapped persons be shown courtesy and given due care, but this emphasis on proper treatment itself indicates their social deprivation.

Among the Dinka physical attractiveness can be other than a gift of God. There is much every Dinka can and does do to enhance an already existing beauty or handsomeness, or to create attraction where there might otherwise be none. Beautification with beads and bangles, make-up with colored ashes and oil, and bleaching the hair reddish or blonde are examples of the preliminaries to full-blown aesthetic display. The most institutionalized forms of this display are singing and dancing. The way the Dinka gratify their inner pride through a song and dance is easily apparent in the way they bear themselves in the process. The elation of spirit and the dignity it gives the dancer are such that a Dinka puts himself into a trance-like condition that is easier felt than described.

Most stories contain dancing and chanted monologues and dialogues. Some storytellers are so inclined to sing while telling stories that they frequently invent situations where singing becomes necessary. In translating the tales, I found the singing so repetitive sometimes that I had to cut the original. Almost invariably, the hero of a tale, who is nearly always the most handsome, is also the best dancer and best singer. His dance qualities are sometimes expressed through the chants with which he accompanies his dancing. As he dances, girls choose to dance with him and the dance group stops to watch him. But singing and dancing are only gestures in an over-all association of aesthetic beauty with movement, and a Dinka is aware that the way he bears himself in his walk, talk, or any other physical activity is as important a consideration as the content of what is conveyed or undertaken.

An extension of these aesthetic concerns are manners—not only the etiquette governing one's behavior towards others but also standards of a personal nature. These are prescribed for all but are more rigorous for men beyond the age of initiation but below old age. The concept of a "gentleman," *adheng*, is very pronounced in Dinka society. Because young men are considered the exemplars of this concept, an initiated young man is referred to as *adheng*. A man should be well-composed, should not wander about in a way that invites invitations, and should not readily accept them. Saying "no" to invitations is practised to the point of hypocrisy.

Even though Dinka spoons are gourds decoratively carved in a way that renders them fragile, a man must be careful not to break one, for that would imply greed. He must take food in small portions and must not empty his plate, however small the portion served. To fill a spoon is a sign of greed. A man must not be near a place where women cook and he himself must never cook or milk except under such exigencies as travel far away from women, and then men must cook and milk for one another and not for themselves. So important is this proscription that coming of age at initiation is sometimes referred to as ceasing to milk cows. Except for cooking and milking, these rules apply to women, although to a less rigorous degree. For instance, unless she is a guest, a woman can break a spoon or empty her dish without shame. But it is much worse for a woman to be greedy in company than it is for a man, and Dinka women are generally very small eaters. As the Dinka put it, "They eat with their eyes." These constraints cannot be explained simply in terms of the need to share food. The Dinka themselves see them as essential rules of dignity.

Although the concept of the gentleman can provide the adult male with "aesthetic" dignity of some importance, the Dinka are aware that the kinds of dignity accessible to youth and women, taken in isolation, are only compensational, that they ameliorate the lack of status attained through material resources. The Dinka word for a person concerned with his appearance and style is *alueeth*, which means "liar." Every young man and every woman is considered to be preoccupied with aesthetic values, and to the Dinka, *alueeth*, as used in this context, is indeed paradoxical praise, befitting the status of these groups.

Dinka awareness of the ambivalences within their concept of aesthetic avenues to dignity is apparent in the stories. These avenues are often presented as fraught with dangers and temptations to err. In *Ajang and His Lioness-Bride* and *Awengok and His Lioness-Bride*, the two most handsome men in the cattle-camp became victims of lioness-girls, also renowned for their beauty. In *Ngor and the Girls*, Ngor's extreme handsomeness and skill in dancing and chanting attracted the girls so strongly that they would impose themselves on him, dance with him, accompany him, and sleep with him. He ate them all, leaving only their heads.

The story of Aluat, who saw beyond Agany's ugly appearance, demonstrates the opposite response—prudence and resistance to the temptations of a superficial concern with beauty. Both the excessive indulgence illustrated in the three lion stories and the humane insights of Aluat's tale indicate that there is a line of demarcation between desirable and destructive aesthetic concern. This line may be determined by the intensity of aesthetic involvement and the degree to which aesthetics are coordinated and balanced with other values. Too intense an involvement may lead to an imbalance and disturb the totality of the Dinka value system. What is desired is an inclusive sense of *dheeng* in which the hero is not only the most handsome, the best dancer, the strongest, and sometimes the richest, but is also notably gentle, conscientious, and a man—or lady—of integrity. The tales advocate the desired balance by dramatizing the temptations of one-sided aesthetic pursuits and their often unfortunate consequences.

## FLIRTATION AND COURTSHIP

The principles underlying the delicate balance of aesthetic or sensual qualities and other values are often presented in these tales within the context of flirtation and courtship. In the way they reveal sexual attractiveness, passion, and the dangers which may result from indiscriminate sexuality, the folktales mirror the subtle attempt the Dinka make to balance freedom of social intercourse between boys and girls and responsible restraint. Girls and boys are presented in the tales as meeting freely in dances and even sleeping together "to converse," a Dinka idiom which normally implies a close relationship between a boy and a girl, involving a degree of sexuality, though not necessarily intercourse. These incidents in the tales mirror the degree of responsible freedom which the Dinka allow their girls. The tales warn against the abuse of such freedom by presenting girls who have involved themselves too deeply in casual relationships as pregnant with the children of strangers, usually lions; and some promiscuous girls are eaten or turned into beasts. In *Ngor and the Girls*, impregnation is said to result from the spit with which lions blessed a kindly, barren woman whose indiscriminate generosity accommodated even craving lions. As usual in such circumstances, the child born of such a casual relationship is a lion.

Proper courtesies, like the respect avoidance of relatives-in-law, are presented as honored by "humans" but disregarded by "lions." These observances are usually associated with respectable marriages; their disregard connotes the abnormalities of animal behavior. Thus, in *Deng and His Vicious Stepmother*, Deng was forced to seek help from his girl friend, but although badly injured, he refused to spend the night in her home and preferred to limp back home before dawn. When Achol tried to persuade him to stay, Deng said, "Do you think I would shame us by staying in your house to be found here in the morning? Of course not. Even if I were dying, I would have to leave before dawn."

It is also customary that a person not eat in the house of a girl he is interested in. Even after marriage, a bridegroom cannot eat the food of his wife's family until certain rites have been performed to break his abstinence. This point is illustrated by *Agany and His Search for a Wife*. Agany refused to drink milk which Aluat, the courteous girl he was to marry, had brought him. Explaining his objection, Agany said to Aluat, "So, take back your milk, my interest in you forbids my drinking it." Again, in *Chol and His Baby-Bride*, Chol moved to the house of the woman who had just given birth to the baby he hoped to raise and marry. Although he lived with the mother and child, taking care of the baby, he would not eat or drink in that house. His water and food were brought from outside the village.

By way of contrast, the lions who made Ngor's mother pregnant with him in *Ngor and the Girls* came into her village and ate with an unusual greed, which made them devour empty gourds. Ngor, one of the offspring of the affair, turned out to be the handsome but wild young man who ate girls until he was forced out of the camp. A more subtle violation of this code is illustrated by *Duang and His Wild Wife*. Amou, who was already betrothed, saw a stranger watching a dance in which she was participating. Attracted by him, Amou aggressively approached him, made friends with him, and invited him home. For two days, Duang lived with Amou's family. She cooked for him and he ate and drank. Earlier his family had urged him to marry, and he had refused on the grounds that he had not yet found the girl of his heart. He married Amou only to find out that she craved meat too much. After a while, he found her intolerable and poisoned her with dog meat. She became rabid, turned wild, and joined the lion world, but was eventually beaten into human form by her brothers and took revenge on her husband.

Amou's unusual aggressiveness, the susceptibility of Duang after waiting so long to find an ideal girl, his violation of the important values of respect for potential relatives-in-law, and his violence against his wife are thus fused together in a course of action which creates the complex, unstated moral of the story.

## FORMALITIES OF MARRIAGE

Private love affairs and marriages undertaken without regard for the views of elders and wider kin bring into sharp focus the individual-group dualism and conflict of agnatic values that operate in Dinka society. For courtship and marriage should be as much group affairs as they are individual affairs. The distinction between individual and group roles is most obvious in the dichotomy between the legal and social formalities of marriage on the one hand, and the winning of the girl's love and affection on the other hand. The former are the functions of elders, and the latter the function of the individual with the assistance of his age-mates. Elders and young men do not always agree. Indeed, their views often conflict.

Both generational conflict and the supporting role of age-mates are well illustrated in *Aluel and Her Loving Father*. There the bridegroom insisted that the bride be brought out from her hiding place to serve his age-set. "The people will neither eat nor drink until the bride comes out to serve! Only when she serves water herself will the gentlemen drink." When the bride's father insisted on hiding his daughter, the bridegroom said: "What cannot be is easily seen—you will not succeed in hiding her. We shall not leave her inside. Please let her come out to serve water to the age-set, so that the people may begin to talk." Acceptance by one's age-mates is important to a proper marriage and can signify, as it seems to in this story, a kind of group approval.

In several of the folktales, the family urges its members to marry, while those members refuse on the grounds that they have not yet found the girls of their own choice. Individual choice is sometimes encouraged for men; girls are generally expected to follow the family's choice. However, even the girls sometimes have their own way, and although the tragedy of the girl in *Atong and Her Lion-Husband* is meant to discourage independent judgment by girls, there are instances when freedom to choose her groom is freely granted a girl. Such is the case in *Ageerpiiu and a Lion*, in which the father, whose supposedly dead daughter returned, refused to give her away solely for cattle. "It is now for my daughter to choose the man of her own heart," he said. "God saved her and sent her back to me, so I will marry her to whomever she wants."

Forcing young people to marry those they do not care for or keeping them from those they want to marry tends to encourage sexual offenses among young Dinkas. Pregnancy or elopement with the loved one is sometimes used to counteract the impediments imposed by the elders. Elders, however, can ignore these obstacles and continue to arrange marriages with other suitors. The offspring of sexual violation may then be forced to go with the mother to the man who eventually marries her. But as is well illustrated by a number of stories (not included in this volume) such children, especially sons, often go back to their biological fathers. Adoption is well established among the Dinka and in stories, it is nearly always the women who are presented as devoted adoptive parents. And since children are often assured of the affection of their natural mothers, it is their return to the biological father that is treated with dramatic intensity, and indeed, advocated in the stories.

Although the theme of delayed marriage focuses on the individual's own sense of romantic involvement, it can also be seen as a subtle way in which society itself conditions young men to be patient and look for a person endowed with greater qualities than a casual infatuation is likely to secure. This way, respect for the mutual affections of the couple and the group's desire to bring an ideal, socially responsible wife into the extended family are fused and balanced.

The need for time to find an ideal wife is only a part of the general Dinka attitude against marrying too early. The collection in this volume cogently substantiates an observation I made independently in an earlier work on the Dinka: "It is generally recognized that boys and girls should experience something of independent life and sexual maturity before they face the responsibilities of married life . . . . Experience and maturity are especially required of men. While it is shameful to remain unmarried for too long, some young men in fact resist early marriage and prefer more of the free unmarried life of the cattle-camp."* This way, independence for the individual and group solidarity, though sometimes conflicting, are delicately accommodated.

---

* Deng, *The Dinka of the Sudan*, p. 27.

## THE FAMILY AND KINSHIP

There is more to the problems of family life than a carefully considered marriage. Polygyny and the way it stratifies people on the basis of sex and age is fertile soil for jealousies, tensions, and conflicts. The intensity with which the stories dramatize the themes of co-wife jealousies indicates how obsessively concerned with them the Dinka are.

The Dinka practice polygyny with an awareness of its negative complications and implications. The major paradox in Dinka family life is the emphasis society places on agnatic continuity and solidarity while knowing the affections between a child and his mother and maternal kin are stronger. A balance is maintained by fostering agnatic solidarity and loyalties as functions of the mind while recognizing maternal sentiments as functions of the heart.

Fostering agnatic solidarity is the primary concern of the tales and the focus is on children, the main treasures of the Dinka, through whom the maintenance of the lineage is guaranteed. Children must receive love and affection from the whole family, no matter whether their relatives are full kin or half kin or even stepkin. The challenge for the half kin and stepkin is usually greater and is, therefore, the theme of most stories. In these stories a woman dies leaving a child under the care of a co-wife. Either immediately or eventually, the child is ill-treated by the stepmother and suffers a great deal, but is eventually rewarded and the stepmother punished.

*Aluel and Her Loving Father* provides an interesting example of how a father should compensate a motherless child for loss of a mother's affection —by controlling a new wife and by showing the child greater love than would normally be given. However, as the story indicates, the balance between the love that a father should show his child and the respect he should maintain for the separate sex roles is a delicate one. Aluel's father, Chol, upset the balance by being so attached to his daughter that he would not permit women, even the child's maternal grandmother, to raise her in the normal fashion; nor would he marry to beget more children for the lineage and to provide his daughter with a mother and perhaps brothers and sisters. His daughter saw this abnormality and argued against it.

Even when he gave in and remarried, Chol continued to be excessively involved with his daughter. This transfer of the love for a wife to a daughter made the second wife jealous, and although she started as a good mother to Aluel, she changed and began to ill-treat her.

Although she appeared to be starving, Aluel never complained about the way her stepmother treated her. That would have violated the Dinka principle that discourages gossiping or backbiting, *lum*, which leads to social disharmony. Respect for this principle is especially important when a relationship involves tensions and potential hostilities. The daughter of the second wife also refrained from reporting her mother to her father, even though she openly criticized her for her treatment of Aluel. In her case, restraint probably stemmed from a combination of Dinka ethics and her own loyalty to her mother.

By transferring love for a wife to his daughter, Chol confused the statuses and roles which Dinka culture carefully defines and abandoned his objectivity and responsibility as a man. So involved with his daughter was he that he would not travel in pursuit of cattle as he would ordinarily be expected to do. Again, it was his daughter who eventually persuaded him to travel, just as she had persuaded him to remarry.

The story breaks the abnormality of the situation by making Aluel disappear as a result of the cruelty of her stepmother. She was adopted by the Sun, who, together with his two wives, showed her much love without confusing roles or statuses and brought her up in  a more congenial atmosphere. Aluel's own ability to balance loyalties—in contrast to her father's inability—appears in her refusal to show preference toward either of the Sun's wives despite constant pressure from them.

When the Sun returned Aluel to Chol, he resumed his possessiveness over the girl and would not let anyone know that she had returned. In those circumstances, she would probably never have married. But she was again saved from abnormality—this time by the intervention of Ring, a young man possessed of mystic powers of perception. Chol accepted his proposal, but found it difficult to part with his daughter and begged to be allowed to satisfy his longing for her. He was eventually dissuaded by the elders of the village, who said to him, "Can't you see that it is God's will that your daughter should not live with you? If God has refused your living with her, then you should surrender and give her to her husband."

But when Aluel got to her marriage home, she was again confronted with a set of complications. This time, the issues were more clearly sexual and involved father-son competition over wives and mother-son attachment.

Father-son relationships among the Dinka are known to involve ambivalences of a love-hate nature. It is the son who succeeds his father to continue the male line. This in itself is a potential threat to the father. As the son matures, marries, and establishes his independence, he symbolizes the end of his father's dominance and perhaps his death. Transfer of control of the family's resources to the son is supposed to take place within the lifetime of the father, provided the son is old enough. But the threats to the father go beyond assumption of his social role by his children and involve a father's fear of his sons taking over his junior wives. Through levirate, they indeed inherit his junior wives to continue begetting children for the lineage in the name of their dead father. In the father's lifetime, however, his wives are sexually exclusive, and there are various rituals of avoidance between sons and their fathers, their mothers, and their stepmothers. To give an example, parents are not supposed to sit on their children's beds. In the case of the father and the mother, the reason is social rather than sexual. A distance between the father and the son minimizes the points of competition and conflict of roles in general. And distance between mother and child restricts maternal influence, which society considers divisive and disruptive. The application of avoidance to stepmothers, on the other hand, is more clearly sexually-motivated. Not only do tensions between senior sons and fathers exist over junior wives (stepmothers), they sometimes result in open conflicts, and are sometimes openly discussed to avoid misunderstandings and discourage violations.

Because of his ambivalent feelings about his son's marriage, Ring's father changed his mind about Ring's marrying Aluel. So he told his son not to consummate the marriage since he, the father, wanted Aluel for himself. The son, of course, found his father's position unacceptable. Finally the father suggested that they should resolve the matter by fighting. He then announced that he would kill his bull to make a shield out of the skin. "It will be for you to decide what you will do—whether to kill your mother to make a shield out of her skin or to go in search of a cow to kill for a shield."

Although the father gives the impression that Ring could find a cow to kill for skin, the story implies that Ring did not really have this alternative; he had to kill his mother or surrender his wife without a fight. This signifies that material resources are controlled by the father. The son who is still dependent on his father cannot acquire wealth and own it independently of his father. Ring, not wanting to kill his mother, decided to surrender his wife to his father.

But his mother overheard the conversation and reproached her son, saying, "Ring, my son, have you always been such a coward? How could you say that you are willing to leave your wife if it requires killing your mother? If you cannot face such a challenge from your father, the man who begot you, of what use can you be?" After a great deal of discussion, Ring was eventually convinced by his mother. Then she said, "When you have slaughtered me, skin me. Make half of my skin your shield and leave the other half. Nobody knows what God will do. You may win your wife. And if you do, use the other half of my skin for sleeping with her."

Ring killed his mother and made a shield from half of her skin. Then he and his father fought under the supervision of Ring's twin brothers, who for days asked them to miss each other, until one lost patience and told his brother to hit their father. So Ring hit him and killed him. As he died, his father said to Ring: "Now that you have killed me, it is fitting that you go with the girl when I am dead. That she should be your wife when I was alive was impossible for me to accept."

Of course, the father's position can be seen as ambivalent. He might have wanted to test the degree to which his son loved the girl, how brave a man his son was, and how great was his willingness to fight and perhaps kill for a principle. All these are values that the Dinka regard highly and inculcate into their children from early years. It is quite apparent that the father died consoled, knowing that he was leaving behind *a man* for his son and heir.

As for the mother's role, it is clearly symbolic of the closeness of the mother-child relationship—how dependent on their children Dinka mothers are for status, how willing they are to sacrifice themselves for their children, and how often they in fact do. It was totally unacceptable to Ring's mother that her son should be humiliated by her husband and she live to see her son's wife turned into her husband's wife. That she was able to influence her son against his own father, her husband, is an example of the divisiveness of women, their power to separate family members and turn them against each other. It is such power that Chol anticipated in *Aluel and*

*Her Loving Father* when he refused to marry, fearing that his wife might treat his motherless child badly and even lead him to turn his back on her. It is because the Dinka are aware of women's jealousies, their divisiveness, and their power to influence men that their personal authority, especially over their own children, is discouraged.

In an effort to suppress the mother's influence over her children, especially sons, most stories put agnatic values above mother-child love. In *Aluel and Her Loving Father*, Aluel's half sister took sides with her against her own mother. Support for the half kin against one's own mother may even lead to the sacrifice of the mother. Thus, in *Deng and His Vicious Stepmother*, the stepmother's natural son, also called Deng, killed his own mother, her brother, and her nephew. The stepmother had initially raised her stepson as her own child, but eventually she had developed an "appetite" for him which led her to pluck a gland from his groin, injuring him badly. Unlike Aluel's stepmother, she is said to be a lioness, perhaps because of the moral gravity of her behavior. When her brother came to revenge her death, his own nephew, her son, killed him. Afraid that his uncle's son might attack him and his half brother, he suggested that they attack first. They did and killed his uncle's son as well.

It is not always true that half brothers and half sisters maintain agnatic solidarity, nor that fathers remain loyal to their motherless children. In *Achol and Her Adoptive Lioness-Mother*, half brothers and sisters deserted Achol and her brother. They were then found by a kindly lioness who took them to safety. Achol's brother ran away, but the lioness raised Achol as her own daughter, and even went to live with her when Achol eventually returned home and married. In *Acienggaakdit and Acienggaakthii*, the motherless Acienggaakthii was ill-treated by everyone, except for one half sister, Ayan, who was married to a lion. Even Acienggaakthii's father turned to his surviving wives and neglected her after her mother's death. In *Wol and Wol After a Lion's Tail*, the motherless Wol could only depend on his married sister and her husband. His father favored him over the other Wol, whose mother was still alive, only after he proved himself more courageous and more dependable than his half brother.

As the mother's sacrifice in Aluel's story indicates, the real, lasting loyalties in the Dinka family are those of the mother and full brothers and sisters. Relations between the child and the father and those between half kin and stepkin can be severed with appropriate rites. But mother-child relations are never severed. A father may curse a child, but a mother is believed to incapacitate herself at her child's birth, so that whatever her anger, she is unable to harm her child through a curse. But because relations between the mother and her child are so close, they threaten wider relationships; they must, therefore, be curtailed. The most dramatic way of curtailing them used in the stories is the child's killing of his own dangerously jealous mother.

There is more to the death of Ring's mother in Aluel's story than self-sacrifice. Her self-sacrifice also effectively removes the potential competition with Ring's wife that might result from her intense love for her son Ring. Such competitions do not seem especially prominent among the Dinka, but it is to avoid potential tensions and conflicts that the Dinka observe strict rules of respect avoidance between relatives-in-law, especially of different generations. The consequences of too much involvement are dramatized in *Nyanbol and Her Lioness Mother-in-law*. Nyanbol's husband had married many girls, all of whom his lioness-mother killed and ate, leaving the skulls hanging in her hut. Nyanbol was saved only through the help of her younger sister and the Palm Tree, the emblem of their clan's deity. Her husband eventually felt compelled to kill his mother.

Another way in which the stories discourage intimacy is shown in their treatment of attempted incest, usually between brother and sister. The attempts are stopped by the killing of the brother who desires the incestuous relationship. Because of the wide circle of relationships which are covered by rules of exogamy, and given the close ties with wider kin and free association between the sexes, Dinka fears of incest involve only distant relationships. Incest within close family circles does not occur and is almost entirely unthinkable to a Dinka. Yet, it is in these circles that tales speak of incest. That they warn against the dangers of such restricted loyalties to encourage wider identification, and yet recognize the sentiments involved, is obvious in *Diirawic and Her Incestuous Brother*. Diirawic's brother failed to marry her; she in fact killed him. But she later adopted as her brother a lion who was turned into a human being through the customary process of physical torture. Through the taming of the lion her own dead brother was symbolically punished and cleansed of his wrong. Diirawic married only when she had seen to it that her adoptive brother married four wives. After Diirawic had borne twelve children, her adoptive brother moved to her village and cleared a field adjacent to her own. Diirawic's thirteenth child displayed the characteristics of a lion. Although her brother wanted the child killed, Diirawic refused, wanting to keep the child. When it became too obvious that the child was a lion, Diirawic's brother killed him. "Then he went and explained to his sister, Diirawic, what he had done." There is no mention of Diirawic's husband in this context and it is difficult not to conclude that despite the original failure of incest, Diirawic eventually committed a form of incest, which might be called social incest.

The story of Diirawic also illustrates a point already made, namely the influence women have despite the alleged dominance of men. Consider, for example, how carefully the balance between the opinions of the paternal kin and the maternal kin is maintained, and even weighted in favor of women and the maternal kin. Diirawic's brother first talked to his mother about his desire to marry his sister. His mother told him to talk to his father. His father told him to talk to his maternal uncle. One of the maternal uncle's first questions was "But what did your mother say about this?" Then he suggested, "I think you should ask your father's sister." The circle went on and although it is not specified, there is reason to think that the logic continued. Eventually, it was the maternal aunt who licensed the marriage, saying, "Marry her if that is your wish. She is your sister." His uncle's saying "if you want my opinion, I think you should ask your father's sister" may indicate the importance of paternal aunts or the independence of that particular aunt and her ability to influence the situation if she were to support her nephew.

The influence of women, sometimes through subversion resulting from their subordination, is also shown in other ways. While Diirawic's sister is presented as a primarily prudent and sympathetic character, it is possible to question her behavior. She appears to be a worrier (probably jealous of her older sister) who actually fans the conflict of the tale. Of course, her constant worry about the lion was prompted by her desire to protect her older sister from the lion who had become infatuated with her. She did not even want her sister to know about the lion. But eventually, she told Diirawic of the lion in much the same way as she had reported her brother's intentions. Diirawic nearly killed the man she was to adopt as a brother because of her sister's information, just as she had killed her own brother under her sister's influence.

Nowhere is the vital role of women in Dinka society better articulated than by Diirawic herself when she explains to the rest of the girls why they were blessed with so much after their flight into the wilderness: "Sisters, we are women and it is the woman who bears the human race. Perhaps God has seen our plight, and not wanting us to perish, has provided us with all this. Let us take it in good grace."

But, of course, Dinka women are aware of the burdens of such a role. Indeed, as I said earlier, Dinka folktales do not, on the whole, have a straightforward, single moral. Quite often, the complexities of real life, the values on which the social relationships are based, the principles by which values are allocated, the injustices implicit in such allocation, and the negative implications of stratification are all fused in a subtle way.

For example, consider *Achol and Her Wild Mother*. The woman should have been wise enough to collect a small bundle of firewood that she could lift by herself since she had no one to help her. In asking a lion to help her, and in return giving him her limbs one by one, the woman was foolish, reckless and too open to strangers, a fault which eventually turns her so wild that she joins the company of lions. Her constant complaint about a load she herself collected contrasts with the behavior of the girl in *Amou and the Son of God*, who labored for her brothers and sisters without complaint or request for help. This not only won her sympathy and help from the girls of the cattle-camp but made the Son of God fall in love with her and marry her. Nevertheless, the suffering of the woman in *Achol and Her Wild Mother* comes through as a call for sympathy. Dinka women usually gather firewood in company in order to assist one another in lifting the loads, but Achol's mother did not have any adult to accompany her in collecting firewood. It would also seem that the absence of her husband from the home, leaving her lonely for him and burdened with the care of the children, is part of what obsessed her even in her wildness. Her first question whenever she returned was "Achol, Achol, where is your father?" She also asked about her two boys, who had gone to the cattle-camp, leaving her with only Achol. Achol continually answered her mother's questions with the word "still"—"still" in the cattle-camp—a response which further illustrates that both Achol and her mother were eagerly awaiting their return. And that the area they lived in was dangerous because of lions was all the more reason for the women not to have been left alone. It could well be that the woman's gift of her limbs to the lion was a form of protection for herself and the children, since the lion might have attacked them otherwise. And the fact that the boys should have gone to the cattle-camp of their maternal relatives, not with their father, would suggest that there was a problem between the father on the one hand and the mother, her relatives, and her children on the other. Indeed, it was not the woman's husband but her son who subdued her and beat her into becoming a human being again.

In another story, *Duang and His Wild Wife*, Amou's craving for meat is portrayed as excessive and unbecoming, especially to a lady. For her lack of self-restraint, her husband eventually poisons her with dog meat. But though Amou's weaknesses indeed call for condemnation, her suffering is also made clear. At the start, it was her real weakness and lack of self-control which made her approach and seduce a man who was merely watching a dance, even though she was already betrothed. However, after the marriage, it is said that while Amou was pregnant with her third child, her husband was in the cattle-camp. He only came home after she had given birth. This was a serious shortcoming on his part; a pregnant woman requires special care and attention. The Dinka believe that meat is an essential part of her diet. Besides, the husband is expected to have sexual intercourse frequently with his pregnant wife in order to "hatch" the baby and facilitate its normal birth and development. Women are indeed said to have a special desire for sex during pregnancy. After birth, sex is supposed to be ended between the parents until the child is weaned. But meat continues to be important for the diet of a newly delivered woman. Thus, Amou was deprived of both meat and her husband's companionship at the crucial period of pregnancy. Lacking self-restraint she craved them excessively after giving birth and probably pushed her husband to the point of intolerance.

When she was poisoned and became wild, her husband left for the cattle-camp with the older boy, leaving their daughter, Kiliingdit, alone with the little baby. As in *Achol and Her Wild Mother*, the area was dangerous because of lions. This was, therefore, serious neglect from the man of the house. Whenever Amou returned, her only question was

"Kiliingdit, Kiliingdit, where has your father gone?" That she was suffering from lack of affection from her husband became most obvious when she suspected that someone other than Kiliingdit must be at home, and Kiliingdit denied the fact. Amou said to her, "Kiliingdit, if your father has returned, why do you hide it from me, dear daughter? Are you such a small child that you cannot understand my suffering?"

Again, as in *Achol and Her Wild Mother*, it is not the husband who beat the lion-woman into becoming a human being again. In this case, it was her brothers. The complexities of the rights and wrongs are substantiated by the fact that her brothers were willing to go to the extreme of killing in retaliation. She refused and returned to him. Apparently now normal in her desires, her husband was very pleased to have her back, but she took vengeance, and somewhat ironically, killed him by feeding him so much food and milk that he burst.

Her refusal to allow her brothers to kill her husband indicates her desire to punish him herself. But it also illustrates the general principle that although relatives should offer aid to their sister if ill-treated by her husband, they should refrain from intervening directly and leave the conflict to the couple as a family affair. Only in extreme cases of maltreatment by the husband are the relatives of the wife expected to intervene in her defense.

Such an extreme is reached in *Atong and Her Lion-Husband*. Atong insisted on marrying only "a man with a bottom lined with a string of shells"—whatever that means. Only a lion could meet this requirement and Atong married him against her brothers' advice. Later the lion held a feast of lions in which Atong was to be eaten. She narrowly escaped and returned home. When her husband came after her, she once more agreed to go back with him, against her brothers' advice. Not convinced about her safety, they followed the couple, hiding themselves from both their sister and her husband. After eating everything his wife had, including her leather skirts, the lion went to the top of a tree, allegedly to pick fruits. He then tried to jump onto her. At the crucial moment, her brothers speared him and killed him. They returned with their sister, and then killed her also.

*Atong and Her Lion-Husband* shows how much Dinka loyalties and their defense are relative to the context. Internal conflicts are to be overlooked when the group is faced with an external threat. Only after an outside challenge is met may internal conflicts be faced, even if they are so grave that their resolution will entail death. Since the lion-husband had proved a vicious outsider, he had to be killed in protection of the sister, whose moral wrong itself deserved the death penalty.

The Dinka view of family loyalty and its rational and emotional dichotomy is aptly illustrated by *The Four Truths*. These truths are presented as: "a wife is a stranger"; "a half brother from a stepmother is a stranger"; "a dog is a loyal friend"; and "a mother's brother is a loyal friend." Those who are said to be strangers are the ones for whom the culture cultivates "rational love," while the loyal friends are those for whom there is natural affection and solidarity. In the story, the man who put people to the test was supposed to be hanged, but eventually people saw his point and he was pardoned. However, it was not for nothing that the story first made him appear to be in the wrong. Dinka affection and solidarity are too complex to be governed by any absolutes. And even though he may have stated the general truth, the man violated the basic demand that although, and probably because, half kin and stepkin solidarities are fraught with jealousies and divisiveness, they must be upheld and advocated above full-blooded loyalties.

## POWER AND LEADERSHIP

Despite the importance of the lineage system among the Dinka, their society is not built solely on kinship and blood ties, for as I have already said, territorial identification is an important part of Dinka social structure. To a certain extent, however, the principles which govern family relationships are projected onto the broader levels of the territory; the chief is, in a sense, the father of the fictionally extended family—the tribe. Just as the father is the worldly representative of the ancestors and the God of the ancestors, the chief is the over-all representative of the great leaders of Dinka history and of the all-embracing God. As the father of the tribe, the chief is the keeper of his people both as a group and as individuals. He must be materially and morally equipped to meet his responsibilities and should, therefore, be the richest, the most righteous, and the most courageous of his tribe—an ideal person in his society. Until modern government ended the practice, the Dinka did not allow their chiefs to die a natural death. Chiefs were buried alive when they were expected to die. The power of the chief was supposed to pass on to his successor, unweakened by the forces of death. He would then remain alive in his people's memory, ruling through his successor, who was usually his son.

For a chief to die meant the diminishing of that vitality from which emanated his divine enlightenment, wisdom, and spiritual power. It was a catastrophe that could break down the society. This is dramatized in *Deng and His Vicious Stepmother* and in *Kir and Ken and Their Addicted Father*. In those stories everyone leaves the cattle-camp because the chief has been killed; their reason is that there is nothing a person can do in a camp or tribe where the chief has been killed.


## AGE-SET SYSTEM

Since the chief did not traditionally possess a police force, his spiritual power was strengthened through the age-set system, which produced warriors to defend the territory from human and animal foes and from deviations by age-mates themselves. Indeed, the age-set system, though reinforced by family ties, is supposed to provide alternatives to total dependence on the family.

Initiation into an age-set subjects young men to severe physical pain, which tests their valor and warrior spirit. To endure the pain of the operation involved means maturity and ability to face the responsibilities of a warrior. But more physical pain follows initiation, in the form of institutionalized fights with age-sets immediately senior to the newly initiated age-sets. While these fights are supposed to train young warriors, they also represent competition between the generations. The usual objects of competition are the girls. The older age-sets try to assert their interest in girls who are now presumably the age-mates and potential brides of the younger generation.

The military role of warrior age-sets, the generational competition of age-sets, and the sexual tensions underlying the competition are illustrated by a number of stories in this volume. In *Awengok and His Lioness-Bride*, the first age-set which went after the lioness to rescue Awengok was the age-set of his father. When "Ayak came running wild to attack the age-set," they ran away in fear and returned home. The age-set below Awengok's father's age-set came next. They, too, were afraid and ran away. Another, younger age-set followed and retreated. Finally, the youngest age-set came. Ayak said to them scornfully, "Do you think that you can do what your elders could not? Do you really think you can defeat me?" The youngest age-set answered her, saying, "We may not be able to defeat you, but we are determined to try." When they nearly killed her, she said, "You have convinced me of your power. Now let me live and I will make him [Awengok] come back to life." They let her live long enough to bring him fully back to life. Then they killed her.

Thus, although the principles of procreation and agnatic continuity subordinate youth to their elders, they can find dignity and gratification in the exercise of their physical strength.

## PROPERTY AND ECONOMY

Another field in which the roles of the generations are clearly marked and in which youth preoccupy themselves with aesthetic or sensual values is the economy. The Dinka are devoted pastoralists, and all Dinka, of course, love cattle and see aesthetic values in them. But it is youth who preoccupy themselves with these aesthetic values. All Dinka also concern themselves with agriculture, but while some young men may be renowned cultivators, it is usually their male seniors and women who do most of the agricultural work, while young men escape to far-off cattle-camps.

Perhaps the aesthetic preoccupation of youth with cattle is best represented by the identification of young men with castrated bulls, which I call personality-oxen. On coming of age at initiation, each man acquires an ox or oxen of a particular color-pattern. The proper color-pattern has long been determined—by his mother's seniority in the family and her son's order of birth. Any ox that accrues to the family belongs to the son whose color-pattern it has. But such ownership does not mean much until initiation, when it becomes active. It is then that a man acquires a metaphoric name based on natural phenomena resembling his ox in color or in shape. As a gesture of intimacy as well as respect, the young man is then referred to by his metaphoric name. The ox is usually decorated with tassels on the horns and a huge bell hanging from a collar tied to the neck. The owner displays the ox, singing ox songs. These may cover a wide range of subjects, but they usually focus on the ox as the symbol of the owner himself and his social standing.

Since they are castrated bulls, oxen symbolize the combination of virility and strength of young men and their subordination and submissiveness to their seniors. In their ox songs, young men admire unruliness and aggressiveness in their oxen even as they superficially condemn them. They sometimes satisfy their aggressive instincts by sharpening the horns of their oxen and bulls and encouraging them to fight with those of rivals. The victory of one's ox or bull over another may be a source of conflict among men, but it is also an occasion of pride and bragging.

The importance of personality-oxen to the identification of a man appears in many contexts in the tales, but it is especially obvious in *Diirawic and Her Incestuous Brother*. Diirawic's brother Teeng sacrificed his personality-ox to celebrate his engagement to his sister, and although such killing of a personality-ox is most unusual among the Dinka, the story makes clear the close association between Teeng and his ox, Mijok. A kite flew down, picked up the tail of Mijok, then flew to the river where Diirawic was fishing and dropped it in her lap. Diirawic did not know that her brother was interested in marrying her and that plans for their engagement were already under way. She recognized the tail and was very disturbed by the thought that Mijok might be dead. Her companions argued that "tails are all the same. But if it is the tail of Mijok, then perhaps some important guests have arrived. It may be that they are people wanting to marry you. Teeng may have decided to honor them with his favorite ox." Diirawic was still disturbed. So she returned home, where she received the news of the intended marriage.

The significance of personality-oxen is, of course, largely symbolic of the importance of cattle to the Dinka and of the special role of youth in the cattle economy. To the Dinka, cattle are much more than a commodity. The fact that they are paid as bridewealth and sacrificed to ensure well-being shows that they are associated with the maintenance of society. Far from the idea of "price," the concept of bridewealth gives cattle something of the emotions involved in the highly valued kinship ties. That bridewealth is collected and shared by a wide circle of relatives means that the cattle help cement the solidarities of kin beyond the immediate families.

In *Chol and His Baby-Bride*, for instance, the girl's father was so pleased that Chol had rescued his daughter from the lioness that he wanted to give her to Chol without bridewealth. "I will not have to be paid any cattle for her marriage," he said. But Chol refused, saying, "This cannot be. It has been a very long time since I first held her and raised her to be a woman. I cannot take her without giving proper payment of cattle. That would be a shame on her and on me. My bringing her from death is small compared to everything else I have intended for her. I must marry her with cattle." It is the fundamental social value found in marriage which associates cattle and youth, for young men are the primary elements in marriage and in the founding of lineages.

Subordinate and aggressive as youth are, their importance for the continuity of the lineage, their pre-eminent role in the cattle economy, and the pervading importance of cattle, even to Dinka concepts of land tenure, all combine to give young men a flattering place in Dinka society. The Dinka words for the various segments of their social structure are largely based on cattle and male youth. Only the term for the family unit composed of a wife, her children, and junior co-wives is based on women, "the front area of the hut," the place where women usually sit in the evening before they retire into the huts for the night. The lineage and the clan are both called "cattle-hearths," a reference to the area around the fire amidst the tethered herds where men and sons gather whether at home or in the cattle-camp. The section, the subtribe, and the tribe are referred to as "cattle-camps," which are usually the domain of youth. Dinka youth, therefore, not only see a vested interest in their one day becoming the elders of the system; they enjoy the fruits of the flattering status of youth. So even if they rebel in various ways (valued by their elders as evidence of the vigor of youth) they basically conform to the system and do not threaten it significantly. Those individuals who rebel excessively, whether by aggressiveness or by violating other precepts of the Dinka code, are considered moral degenerates. In the folktales, they are usually the ones who turn into lions.

The Dinka are aware that excessive violence, whether directly expressed by youth in wars or sublimated through oxen and bulls, is a means of compensating for disadvantages and deprivations. They believe that it is often the weak and the powerless who make loudest claims to strength and are more aggressive. Unless provoked, the courageous and the strong are usually gentle and passive. This is pertinently illustrated by the Dinka belief that hornless cattle, which are obviously ill-armed, are usually more aggressive and dangerous than cattle with horns. In a number of stories included in this volume, when lions' cattle are captured, men take only the cattle with horns, and the hornless cattle become wild, turn into lions, and disappear with their defeated masters. In view of the close identification of human beings with cattle and the sublimation of men's aggressiveness through bulls, it is easy to see how this symbolism applies to human relationships. One can expand the analogy to say that violation of the moral code, which in the stories leads to the culprit's expulsion from human society until beaten back into human form, implies moral weakness and susceptibility to evil rather than superiority to community standards. If physical weakness can produce excessive aggressiveness in cattle, moral weakness can produce deviance from the norms of human relationships.


## RELIGION AND WELL-BEING

It is quite fitting that the Dinka should symbolize moral degeneration by transformation into animals, and correction by beating; for their religion is worldly based and concerns itself with the practical welfare of man in society rather than with a heaven and hell to come after death. So rooted in the basic realities of life is their view of God that while they believe God is One, He is conceived of in lineage terms—as "God of my Father" or "God of my Ancestors." That a Son of God should attend an ordinary dance in *Amou and the Son of God* and marry a girl in an ordinary Dinka way reflects this conception.

Despite man's attempt to establish familial ties with God, the Dinka conceive of Him as distant and little involved with men. So they recognize a variety of spirits, sometimes symbolized by natural phenomena, as protectors and intermediaries with God. An example of the role of such spirits can be drawn from *Nyanbol and Her Lioness Mother-in-law*. In that story Nyanbol prayed to the Palm Tree, the emblem of her clan's spirit, to bend in order for her to climb to safety. When she climbed, the tree straightened up again. Its spiritual power made it impossible for the mother-in-law to cut it down.

Various spiritual practices are illustrated in a number of stories in which medicines are used for evil or for good. Sometimes, as in *Ayak and Her Lost Bridegroom*, medicine is used for drugging a person into unconsciousness so that he or she may then be carried away. But in that story, Ayak is also given a medicine which can both kill and restore life. In *Kir and Ken and Their Addicted Father*, an invisible magical stick takes the place of lethal medicine.

The notion that divination and expulsion of evil can restore health underlies the process of re-creation which always follows death or injury in the tales. The stepmother in *Deng and His Vicious Stepmother*, when confronted by her son, restored the gland she had plucked from his half brother's groin and healed the wound. In *Ayak and Her Lost Bridegroom*, *Ajang and His Lioness-Bride*, and *Awengok and His Lioness-Bride*, dead persons are brought back to life when evil is challenged.

In *Ayak and Her Lost Bridegroom*, the lioness is first killed, brought back to life, and is again killed after restoring Ayak's husband, this time never to be brought back to life. Even when they revive people they have victimized, lions are never pardoned; they are invariably put to death. But human beings who turn into lions and are beaten into human form again are accepted and integrated into society. In all cases, such people become lions by turning wild but do not eat human beings. Their punishment is, therefore, primarily rehabilitation; they have not gone beyond hope.

But even though a lion who has killed a person is punished by death, some kind of reconciliation takes place beforehand, and the dying lion blesses the man or woman restored to life with many children. This kind of resolution is the outcome of an impulse described elsewhere to explain some of the mythicized incidents in the history of clans. "In these legends, the Dinka try to create a protective relationship out of a destructive experience. The evil and the good aspects of the experience are merged into a positive image, and the object and the subject of the experience are reconciled as relatives who must no longer antagonize one another, but must indeed assist each other."*

* Deng, *The Dinka of the Sudan*, p. 123 (1972).

By reconciling himself with a lion he has just mortally wounded, a man justifies his act, clears his conscience, and makes the memory positive. In *Chol and His Baby-Bride*, the lioness who had just been killed addressed Chol as she died, saying, "I knew you would take my life. I knew you would kill me. This girl will go with you. She will be your wife. Nothing else will befall her. In the future, when you are husband and wife, she will bear children—many children. Her children alone will be enough to hold a dance. Your first-born will be a girl. When she marries, take a small calf, raise it to be known as mine. If it is slaughtered for me, that too would be good. That will guarantee good health for you and your children and will make your wife produce many children." Chol said, "We shall do as you say," and went ahead and gave her a death blow. When their first daughter was married they dedicated the calf to the lioness, and Chol's wife "continued to bear children; so many that her children were enough to complete a dance all alone." In *Ayak and Her Lost Bridegroom*, a lioness again blessed a couple with children, but also condemned the parents to die together when their eighth child was born.

Another way in which guilt is removed appears in *Deng and His Vicious Stepmother*. In that story, whenever the two brothers killed a person, they burnt their victims and threw black rams into the burning fire for sacrifice. That way, they reconciled themselves symbolically with the burning victim and satisfied their conscience.

These ways of removing guilt accord well with Godfrey Lienhardt's explanation of Dinka religion in his book *Divinity and Experience, Religion of the Dinka*.* According to him, the Dinka memory of an experience is projected from the mind of the remembering person to form an image that acts upon him from outside himself. What Westerners call "memories" of experience and consider intrinsic and interior to the person remembering—and therefore modified as part of the remembering person—are seen by a Dinka as apart from the remembering person and a part of the external sources from which they originate. They continue to act upon him as did the sources themselves. Divine essence is attributed to this externalized image, which is understood by the remembering person to be capable of making demands or of conferring benefits.

* Oxford: Clarendon Press (1961). See especially p. 149.

Lienhardt's distinction between interiority and exteriority should be understood to assume that although the image takes on an exterior appearance, the fact that it originates within the experiencing person and exerts influence on him shows a unity between *him* as the object and the image as the subject. Indeed, the identities of subject and object become so interfused that at a certain point it is no longer possible to distinguish them, and to that extent, Lienhardt's distinction may seem a matter of labels. The West may speak of "conscience," the Dinka of spirit, but both are essentially the same.

Nonetheless, the distinction is significant, because a Dinka who deals with his conscience as an image or a spirit outside himself is able to resolve issues with it more easily than a man who associates himself consciously with the remembered experience. The resolution is made particularly easy by the fact that all the cards are in the hands of the remembering person; the exterior image is in his memory and is, therefore, part of him, and yet outside him. This ambivalence of the image facilitates his manipulation of the situation. One may, therefore, hypothesize that through symbolic action, a Dinka is more easily able to rid himself of guilt than a Westerner. Such symbolic action to remove guilt seems to function—below the conscious level—in *Diirawic and Her Incestuous Brother*. After killing her brother, Diirawic fled her home; only after she had adopted another brother did she return. Expiation through symbolic action is not unique, of course, to the Dinka. Confession and penance among the Catholics would seem to be a form of sacrifice to remove guilt and an attempt to turn a bad experience into a positive relationship.

The memory of an experience does not always take the form of a demand for sacrifice to expiate guilt. A man may honor good experience by repaying his benefactor in the form of sacrifice, as happened in *Aluel and Her Loving Father*. When the Sun brought Aluel back, he said to her father, "When this daughter of yours gets married, take a brown calf and tether her to a peg very early in the morning. I will pick up the cow-calf on my way to the West." Not to honor such an experience is supposed to bring a curse on the defaulting person, for just as sacrifice turns a bad experience into a positive relationship with the remembered object, failure to honor a remembered virtuous object turns it into a spiritually dangerous one. Even in ordinary human situations, a person who has done a significant favor for a girl must receive a share in her bridewealth; otherwise some misfortune, such as childlessness or her children's death, befalls her.


## SOCIAL CHANGE

The occasional humanization of the animals, notably lions, in the tales reflects Dinka attempts to tame dangerous creatures by making them "relatives" and integrating them into their world. As dangerous animals become totems, so lions become human—and the value system of the Dinka is secured from non-conformity and can continue largely unchanged. I have already speculated that the so-called lions of the stories are people (or attributes of people) who fall out of harmony with the basic tenets of the Dinka code. I have also said that this view of human beings as lions is particularly applicable to outsiders, the obvious agents of social change.

The only exception to the total disregard of foreigners in folktales is *Thaama and Mohammed*. In that story, Mohammed, a judge of importance and presumably an Arab, pursued Thaama, a beautiful black girl. Thaama was renowned for being difficult to procure; that made Mohammed even more determined to have her. Thaama tricked Mohammed into thinking that she had slept with him; in fact, it was Thaama's female slave with whom he had slept. Offended by this trickery, Mohammed succeeded in procuring Thaama as his wife by paying her family many cattle. But he then retaliated against Thaama by giving her to his black slave. Thaama persuaded the slave not to touch her, explaining her background and how she had come into the house believing herself married to Mohammed. She eventually played another trick on Mohammed by bribing his wife with beautiful plates to sleep with the slave, while she, Thaama, slept with Mohammed. This was not known to Mohammed. Both women became pregnant; Mohammed's wife bore a black son, while Thaama had a very brown son. When the matter was eventually explained to Mohammed, he gave his wife to the slave and took Thaama for his wife. Thaama's story is of rather dubious origin, but it throws some light on both the traditional Dinka view of the outsider and the exigencies of changing Dinka society today.

The Dinka have been traditionally resistant to change, though they have selectively adopted elements of foreign culture and assimilated them into their own culture. A classical example of this selection is their adoption of the Islamic religious concept of the Mahdi while successfully resisting northern rule under the leadership of the religious nationalist, the Mahdi, whose rise introduced the concept to the Dinka. The Dinka composed hymns praising the spirit, Mahdi, as the son of Deng, an important deity, and imploring his help against the man, Mahdi, the northern leader. Evidence of such adoption and assimilation of elements of alien culture appears in *Kir and Ken and Their Addicted Father, Wol and Wol After a Lion's Tail,* and *The Four Truths,* in which horses, police, and lawful executions are mentioned as though they were indigenously Dinka, although they came to the Dinka through the Arabs and the Europeans in the relatively recent past.

That the Arabs and the Europeans, the source of these elements, are not mentioned in the tales can also be explained by history. Until the British came to put an end to slavery, Dinka contact with the outsider was, for the most part, hostile. The outsider was hardly human then and to see him as a lion was particularly congenial to the Dinka mind. Consider, for example, *Kir and Ken and Their Addicted Father.* Although it has often been said that the Dinka never took "to the vile, but common, practice of selling their fellow tribesmen into slavery,"* the need to discourage the possible occurrence of such vile practices could give rise to such a story. The idea of a desperate man being tempted into surrendering his children for material gain is not inconceivable, especially in view of the famines that were said to accompany the destruction of invasion. That the father in the tale was addicted to tobacco may only be a symbolic way of emphasizing the compelling circumstances of the time. It is interesting, too, that after defeating the lions, Kir and Ken rode home on bulls, a practice which still exists among the Arabs. Although the Dinka ride Arab bulls which have been trained as animals of burden, they do not use their own cattle that way. So the boys' ride suggests that the cattle-camp which they captured was an Arab camp.

With the intervention of the British and the establishment of a peaceful context for interaction with outsiders, the Dinka view seems to have changed to the point where foreigners were no longer viewed as lions *per se,*

* G. W. Titherington, "The Raik Dinka," *Sudan Notes and Records,* 10 (1927) p. 169.

though, of course, the lion-characterization of the moral drop-out might still apply to particular outsiders as it would to individual Dinka. It is perhaps in this context that *Thaama and Mohammed* can be explained.

It is possible that although the story is told by a Dinka, the facts from which it originated are Northern Sudanese and concern the process of assimilating those southerners who were enslaved and brought to the North. For one thing, the name "Thaama," though not noticeably Arab, is not Dinka either. For another, the story was told by a girl in a Northern Sudanese town. Even the way she introduced the story, "This is an ancient event, a story which used to be told in the ancient past when people played by telling stories," would seem to suggest that she had fallen out of the practice of telling bedtime stories because she lived under northern conditions.

Whether it is authentically Dinka or rooted in early processes of assimilation in the North, the story is relevant to the current realities of Dinka social change and migration to northern towns. Migration first began with young men who saw in the modern market an opportunity for independent wealth. Within the tribe, there is no paid labor. But more important, because of the Dinka's intense pride, paid labor is seen as servility and is regarded as inappropriate for a gentleman. Therefore, it must be carried out far away from the Dinka girls and in a country where it will not matter. The saying goes, "Dignity, remain, indignity let us go"— which means pocketing pride in a foreign land where one is unknown. It is also said that "a gentleman of one tribe does not know a gentleman of another tribe." That is, one is not fully recognized in a foreign land and the rules of dignity do not apply strictly there. But for the Dinka, the conflict between the material advantage of the town and loss of the dignity of their traditional status poses serious dilemmas.

Recently migration has affected girls and families. Women are generally employed in homes under more comfortable and respectable conditions than their male counterparts, an arrangement which permits them to adapt more easily to the new environment. But to the Dinka, the result is often not so respectable as it may seem. Dressed in Arab clothes and proficient in Arabic, superficially integrated into employing families but lacking adequate supervision and cultural restraints, young girls grow up in an atmosphere of permissiveness and perhaps promiscuity. The pressures in favor of their becoming mistresses to their employers are great and sometimes irresistible. They come to acquire wealth to help their relatives subsist and perhaps buy cattle, but often they return worthless for Dinka marriage. Usually there is "their kind" to marry them, but even then these are only "limping" marriages.

Thaama's story can be seen, therefore, both as a reflection of current realities and an attempt to uphold the standards that the Dinka desire their youth to observe in the process of cross-cultural interaction. Both the male slave and Thaama may be Dinka, and both ultimately seem to marry into a good circle in northern society. In effect, the story yields to the need for integration, but sanctions it only on the basis of social and cultural equality between the northerner and the Dinka.

# Recording Dinka Folktales

## Sources

| TALE | TELLER | AGE | SEX | AFFILIATION |
|---|---|---|---|---|
| 1. *Aluel and Her Loving Father* | Nyanjur Deng | 20+ | F | Daughter of Paramount Chief Deng Majok |
| 2. *Deng and His Vicious Stepmother* | Nyanjur Deng (see 1) | | | |
| 3. *Agany and His Search for a Wife* | Amou Bol | 40+ | F | Wife of Chief Deng Majok and Nyanjur's mother |
| 4. *Chol and His Baby-Bride* | Nyanjur Deng (see 1) | | | |
| 5. *Diirawic and Her Incestuous Brother* | Unknown | 20+/− | M | Unknown |
| 6. *Kir and Ken and Their Addicted Father* | Unknown | Unknown | F | Unknown |
| 7. *Achol and Her Wild Mother* | Nyankoc Deng | 18–20 | F | Daughter of Chief Deng Majok and wife Alang |
| 8. *Duang and His Wild Wife* | Nyanjur Deng (see 1) | | | |
| 9. *Nyanbol and Her Lioness Mother-in-law* | Unknown (see 6) | | | |

| TALE | TELLER | AGE | SEX | AFFILIATION |
|---|---|---|---|---|
| 10. *Ayak and Her Lost Bridegroom* | Nyanbithou | 13+/− | F | Granddaughter of Chief Deng Majok |
| 11. *Ajang and His Lioness-Bride* | Nyanjur Deng (see 1) | | | |
| 12. *Awengok and His Lioness-Bride* | Unknown | 20+ | M | Unknown |
| 13. *Achol and Her Adoptive Lioness-Mother* | Unknown | 20+ | F | Unknown |
| 14. *Ageerpiiu and a Lion* | Kwol Deng | 10+/− | M | Son of Chief Deng Majok |
| 15. *Amou and the Son of God* | Unknown | 20+ | M | Unknown |
| 16. *Wol and Wol After a Lion's Tail* | Unknown | 20+ | M | Unknown |
| 17. *Atong and Her Lion-Husband* | Nyankoc Deng (see 7) | | | |
| 18. *The Four Truths* | Adut Kwel | 20+ | F | Unknown |
| 19. *Ngor and the Girls* | Adau | −10 | F | Daughter or granddaughter of Chief Deng Majok |
| 20. *Acienggaakdit and Acienggaakthii* | Peter Akol | 30+ | M | Member of Apuk tribe, chiefly lineage |
| 21. *Thaama and Mohammed* | Adut Kwel (see 18) | | | |

AS I HAVE ALREADY NOTED, most of the tales in this volume were recorded for me by my brother Biong and cousin Kwol, and although I do not know some of the people who told the stories, most of them are members of our family, a family so large and extended that my research assistants, as I said earlier, had to travel long distances from town to town and from one settlement to another collecting stories.

Amou Bol, a middle wife of my father in her forties, told the story of *Agany and His Search for a Wife*. Nyanjur, her eldest child, a girl in her early twenties, told five stories: *Aluel and Her Loving Father*, *Deng and His Vicious Stepmother*, *Chol and His Baby-Bride*, *Duang and His Wild Wife*, and *Ajang and His Lioness-Bride*. Another sister, Nyankoc, a girl in her late teens, told *Achol and Her Wild Mother* and *Atong and Her Lion-Husband*.

Of the remaining storytellers, the names of some were recorded with the tales, but in some cases no name was given at all, or if given, no elaboration on family affiliation was provided. A child who, judging from her voice, must be below ten years of age told the story of *Ngor and the Girls*. Her name, Adau, is a typical Pajok clan name and it is easy to surmise that she is my half sister or niece. Nyanbithou, another niece who must be in her early teens, a daughter of my older half sister, told *Ayak and Her Lost Bridegroom*. Kwol, a small half brother of about ten years of age, told the story of *Ageerpiiu and a Lion*.

Of the remaining stories, two, *The Four Truths* and *Thaama and Mohammed*, were told by a girl called Adut Kwel who has some distant affinity with the family but is unrelated by blood. The story of Diirawic was told by a young man whose name and family background is unspecified. The same is true of the young men who told the stories of *Awengok and His Lioness-Bride*, *Amou and the Son of God*, and *Wol and Wol After a Lion's Tail*, and of the girls who told the stories of *Kir and Ken and Their Addicted Father*, *Nyanbol and Her Lioness Mother-in-law*, and *Achol and Her Adoptive Lioness-Mother*. The story of *Acienggaakdit and Acienggaakthii* was told by Peter Akol of the chiefly lineage of Apuk in the Rek group of tribes.

Thus, at least eleven stories were told by members of one immediate family, six of them by one woman and her daughter. Less than a third of the stories were told by men—all of whom were children or young men; the rest were told by women, mostly small girls or young women. From what we have said about the institution of storytelling, it is easy to understand why it is mostly women and young people who tell the stories. Stories tend to be associated with bedtime and are geared towards the children, who usually sleep with women, the primary educators of early childhood. The fact that most of the stories were recorded within one kinship circle is obvious. But more should be said about the significance of this family circle as a mirror of Dinka culture.

It should be pointed out that the leading Ngok family, whose members told many of these stories, is exceptional not only in its cross-cultural linkage of the Arab North and Negroid South, but also in its size. It is customary among the Dinka for a chiefly family to be the largest in the tribe. The chief is often the wealthiest member of the tribe and therefore can afford to procure the largest number of wives. His political responsi-. bilities necessitate diplomatic marriage into the widest possible circles within his immediate tribe and neighboring tribes to strengthen his base of power and to reinforce his symbolic image as the head of the fictionally extended family, the tribe. The late Chief Deng Majok of the Ngok extended the practice of diplomatic marriage farther than anyone else in the history of the Dinka. He had nearly two hundred wives, drawn from most of the corners of Dinkaland. And unlike other chiefs, who in the Dinka fashion disperse their wives' settlement, Chief Deng's family was closely knit, living in several large villages. As a result of the diversity of its members, within his family all kinds of dialects were spoken and all kinds of Dinka subcultures were reflected. As the main meeting place of the tribe, a Dinka chief's home has the advantage of absorbing a wide range of sources of information and cultural expression. Amou, who together with her daughter told six of the stories in this volume, came from the Ruweng of Upper Nile Province and it may well be that the stories she and her daughter told emanated from that context. Although the established family tends to remold the people it affiliates or admits, it is fair to say that a chief's family and in particular, the Ngok chief's family, represents a microcosm of the Dinka.

Nonetheless, it is in the nature of Dinka stories to be reshaped to suit the particular dynamics of the context in which they are told. It is therefore natural that stories told by members of such a large family would give special attention to the complexities of polygyny—jealousies, tensions, and conflicts—together with the ideals the society postulates to harmonize relations between family members—communalism, family solidarity—and the stringent measures it takes against those who violate the moral code. In view of their character as an expression of social realities, it is also natural that the stories should reflect the particular social context and personal attributes of the storyteller. To give one example, Amou is a woman who is known for her charm, intelligence, tact, and gentle feminine style. She was certainly one of the most favored wives of my father. It is also quite obvious that her children have acquired her positive attributes to a striking degree. For those who know them it is easy to see these qualities reflected in the way they tell stories. Many people who have listened to their tales on tapes enjoyed listening to them even though they did not know the language. It does not require farfetched speculation to see in both the substance of the stories and their form of delivery the qualities possessed by Amou and her daughter, and through those qualities the underlying realities of the world to which these women respond. Nor is it surprising that a personality of great intelligence, charm and gentle style should be drawn to stories that include complex social relationships and cold-blooded brutality. In story form, the complex and sometimes harsh realities of the Dinka world can be explored dramatically and with some freedom, perhaps a necessity in passing on penetrating and affecting knowledge of the social milieu in which storyteller and audience must live.

Although the full value of these tales—especially for anthropology—may not be derived until they are compared with others from more varied sources, I have found it challenging and worthwhile to relate their literary and cultural characteristics and the complexities of their content to the social and individual backgrounds of the people who told them. The challenge now extends to collecting additional stories from further sources and making comparative analyses of both literary quality and social content.

## Translation

In translating Dinka folktales, I tried to be loyal to the Dinka manner of expression without sacrificing clarity too much. The fact that the tales were transcribed from tapes compounded the problem of translation, so I could not always conform rigidly to the Dinka construction.

The translations, for one reason or another, reveal symbolic meanings which would not be apparent in Dinka. To take one area as an example, a great deal of sexual symbolism, which may be inherent or implicit in the Dinka original but is not viewed as such by the Dinka, suddenly becomes very prominent in English. It is tempting to see sex and incestuous desire in expressions such as one used in *Deng and His Vicious Stepmother:* "Deng of the lioness had observed his mother lately and had noticed a change in her. It was as though she was developing an appetite for the human Deng." The same is true of her plucking a gland from the groin of her stepson, an act which seems to suggest sexual desire and castration. In *Ngor and the Girls*, how can one avoid the sexual significance of Ngor being so attractive to girls that they followed him, slept with him, and *he ate them all*, leaving only their heads? Even a practice like homosexuality, or more pertinently in this context, lesbianism, behavior unknown to the Dinka, seems to emerge in the passage in *Chol and His Baby-Bride* describing the lioness' infatuation with the human girl, Atholong: "She was so attracted by the girl that whenever she wanted to eat her, she would look at her and change her mind and say, 'O, what beauty; I will eat her tomorrow.' She would then go and hunt for animal flesh.... She kept coming back to attack her, but each time she would put off Atholong's death, saying, 'There is just one more thing to do. Let me pile up more grass so that the sand does not touch her beautiful skin. Perhaps I should find something even smoother to lay her on as I eat her.' ... The lioness went and cut some more grass to put on top of the platform to make it even more comfortable."

To a Dinka, however, Deng's lioness-mother was simply vicious, and plucking the gland from Deng's groin was merely indicative of her cannibalistic tendency. Ngor was a young man who had inherited animal qualities from his mother's wild suitors, one who abused his attractiveness to girls by eating them. The lioness's infatuation with Atholong is simply natural appreciation of beauty, not lesbian attraction. Indeed, the Dinka tend to take the tales at their face value and do not probe to see their symbolic importance.

The difference between the Dinka view of the tales as expressed in Dinka language, and what we may call the Western view, reflected in the English translation, may be representative of the difference between folk cultural outlook and a scientific, analytical view. Dinka as a language still represents the former, while English now tends to represent the latter, although needless to say, there are English-speaking folk societies whose attitude to the tales might approximate the Dinka approach, just as there are Dinka who have adopted the analytical approach.

Nonetheless, the dichotomy remains culturally and linguistically significant. I once tested a group of educated Dinka by having them listen to the following story in Dinka and then read its translation in English.

There were two stepsisters, Achol Aretret, that is, the unruly Achol, and Achol Adheng, the gentle Achol. Achol Aretret was very disobedient and ill-mannered. Achol Adheng was her opposite. One night they heard drums beating, and Achol Aretret suggested that they attend the dance. Against the advice of elders and Achol Adheng, she insisted. So they went. The dance was a mixed human-lion dance. They danced with two lions, Lual and Lual, who were stepbrothers. One Lual was vicious, and the other gentle. As Dinka girls choose their dance-mates, Achol Aretret chose to dance with the vicious Lual. As they danced, the vicious Lual started to turn wild, and as his tail and fur emerged, his stepbrother warned him in a dancing *mioc*.*

"Lual of my father,
O Lual of my father,
Beware of the Dinka girl."
The vicious Lual answered:
"O Lual, my brother,
*Dheeng* has excelled.
Achol does not know the words;
Achol who does not know the words,
Where have you come from?
I shall eat her
Between the upper hut and the pillar."
The gentle Achol noticed what was happening and warned her sister,
"Daughter of my father
Where goes the long tail?"
Her sister answered,
"Isn't the tail the sign of beauty?
For a tail, a girl will choose a man.
He came with black hair,
The hair on his head heavy and thick."

---

* *Mioc* is a poetical exclamation which can accompany one's dance.

After the dance, the two men escorted the girls home, and as they entered the hut, the vicious Lual seized Achol Aretret, and ate her.

The members of the group I tested agreed that the translation was accurate, yet they saw a great deal of sexual symbolism in the translation which they thought totally lacking in the Dinka version. In Dinka, Lual is simply a vicious lion-man capable of changing form whenever his lion instinct is aroused by his desire for meat.

Even though individual educated Dinkas are able to see symbolism in the words of a tale, the general tendency of the Dinka, uneducated and educated alike, is to remain unconscious of the hidden realities with which the tales are concerned. The tales themselves would seem, then, to exert their influence on Dinka and Western readers in different ways. And, indeed, one well-educated Dinka reading a few samples of the stories in this collection reacted by saying, "What I don't like about Dinka stories is that they embody a great deal of rubbish which is not relevant to the real world. It is, for instance, nonsensical to make animals communicate with people."

As an outcome of this Dinka approach to tales, we may expect that for some time to come books of folktales will not appeal to Dinka readers as much as they will to Westerners. For a Dinka, stories are for children and to some extent women, who often tell them to children. Adults must concern themselves with reality. Indeed, I recall losing interest in fiction in my mid-teens once I realized that it did not reflect "real events." I wondered why fiction writers treated us readers as children. It was not until much later in my life that I began to see the reality within fiction. It is, perhaps, completing this cycle which has enabled me to see reality in the fantasy of Dinka tales.

Because I now realize their relevance to a deeper understanding of life, I have attempted in my commentary to place the tales in as comprehensive a context and as close to the Dinka's own view of their culture as possible. But it is perhaps important to stress that not all my analytical observations would be obvious to the traditional Dinka. Of course, I have not attempted to be exhaustive in my analysis of the folktales. I have merely tried to illustrate for the reader their relevance to Dinka values and institutions. My primary objective has been to present the tales, and I believe they stand on their own. For the curious reader, I hope my commentary will provide a useful framework for understanding the complexities and the subtleties behind what I, for one, have found to be on the whole fascinating stories.